BLEED FOR THE BROTHERHOOD

THE ILLICIT BROTHERHOOD

BLEED FOR THE BROTHERHOOD

THE ILLICIT BROTHERHOOD

GAIL HARIS // ASHTON BROOKS

Bleed for the Brotherhood
By Gail Haris and Ashton Brooks

Note: This story may not be suitable for persons under the age of 18.

Cover: Lou Stock
Photographer: Wander Aguiar
Model: Lucas Loyola
Formatting: Elaine York- Allusion Publishing (http://www.allusionpublishing.com)

Trigger Warning

Bleed for the Brotherhood is a dark college romance that contains explicit sexual content, graphic language, and some situations that readers may find uncomfortable, such as blood, murder, death, self-harm, violence, snakes, and alligators. We hope you enjoy this secret society of possessive alphas and the women keeping them in check.

ACKNOWLEDGEMENTS

Thank you for taking time to read *Bleed for the Brotherhood! We hope you loved it.* We know your time is precious, and we appreciate you spending it with these characters. All the answers you have been waiting for are coming soon as the world of the Illicit will either unravel or grow stronger.

Thank you, Elaine, for tolerating us and helping us with this project. Even if we have a crisis you are nothing but great to us. We appreciate all your hard work — your support is EVERYTHING!

Brenda, thank you for jumping in and giving us your time and hardwork. We are grateful for you and all that you do for us.

Lou...for the amazing work she does on our covers!! You're an artistic genius! LOVE YOU!

Thank you to our beta readers: Rachael, Lori, and Stephanie.

We'd never have made it this far if not for our incredible support system: our incredible and dedicated PAs, Carolina and Lori — the freakin' best team ever, the most epic street teams, our reader groups, the most incredible group of friends: Shucky Darn Crew: Sara, Rachel, Katie, Amanda (tits), and Lori – **who we'd all be lost without!**

Special shout out to our wonderful families who continue to inspire us every single day!

Enjoy the Brotherhood...the end is near...

XOXO

Ashton & Gail

THE ILLICIT BROTHERHOOD GLOSSARY

The Illicit Brotherhood: A secret society of elite powerful members. Members are intertwined through high social positions and the underground world of crime. All are wealthy and extremely dangerous. There is a president and every family picks a 'head' to represent them at meetings.

Founding Families: The original founding families are: Suco, Concord, Carmichael, Boudreaux, Van Doren, and Dupree.

Original Bloodline: This refers to descendants of a founding family. Killing a member from an original family is a harsh offense. It must be voted on between head family members. If a family does something to disgrace or go against The Illicit, one remaining heir may live and strive for repentance.

Delta Pi Theta: A social fraternity at Thorn University, in Blue Rose, Alabama. This fraternity is the training base for the future of The Illicit Brotherhood. Founding families send their male heirs to rush this fraternity. The brotherhood also grows through new members and molds them to fit The Illicit. They form bonds within the brotherhood and establish their roles.

Scabs: Pledges of Delta Pi Theta

The Blue Tie: Delta Pi Theta brothers wear royal blue ties to all meetings and social functions. If a brother becomes serious about having a partner and bringing them into the know of The Illicit Brotherhood, they give them their blue tie. This lets everyone know not to pursue the person as they are 'claimed.'

JOURNAL ENTRY

Unknown author

Drip. Drip. Drip.

Rip. Rip. Rip.

They think they've won.

They think they are close, but they will never catch me.

Not the Carmichaels, certainly not the Concords. They're all so enamored by their Little Mouse, they will never know the real threat is already in their home.

The blood has already been spilled.

CHAPTER ONE

Thorn University

Lee

My sister is gone. No, she was taken. It hasn't been more than twenty-four hours since the discovery, but my hopes are hanging on by a thread. With everything that has been going on at the campus, and the direct threat to The Illicit, I know Chanda's disappearance is intentional. Our father tried to laugh it off as her wanting attention, or having her phone somewhere and just not answering . I didn't trust him enough to confide in him that her phone was found, shattered, among the disarray that suggested a struggle ensued. I can't imagine my sister not putting up a fight, and that thought would make me laugh if the situation weren't so dire. I can only hope that she is giving hell to the person who was foolish enough to take her.

"Any news?" Steffan's voice is low as his hand claps me on the shoulder. I shake my head no in response, glancing down at my phone, again, willing it to ring. Jose went ballistic when he heard the news. Soren had to remind him, before he left the house, that not only was his initiation on the line, but also Chanda's life. If he wanted the help of The Illicit at all, the elders were not going to want to know that she was in a relationship with a Scab. Anyone with eyes could clearly see how he was affected. Part of me knows Chanda deserves to be loved correctly, while another part of me disagrees that Jose Succo is the man for the job. Only time will tell, I guess.

"Jose hasn't responded. His unit was doing perimeter checks around town. My dad said if we can find a shred of evidence she isn't in town, he will speak to the elders," I gave him the information before taking a drink of the amber liquor in my glass. The internal war in me continues to rage constantly, and only drinking has helped me so far. Well drinking and her...but that isn't a topic I can think about right now.

"We'll find her," Steffan assures me, and I wish I had his optimism at this point. Nothing with any of these killings has made sense, except for the fact that it is very apparent whoever the murderer is, they want members of The Illicit.

Give the killer my father. *Protect the elders.*

Make them all pay. *Value the Brotherhood.*

Burn this town to the ground. *You have alliances.*

The war rages on and on until it creates a buzzing noise in my mind. I jump from the chair, the need to move, to be useful, overtaking me. The fraternity house, that used to be my safe haven, has become a form of torture. The lines of right and wrong blur every time I walk in the door. "What if she ends up like the others?"

Images of snakes slithering out of bodies, skin flayed off human backs to look like angel wings, and the vacant, gaping holes in the chests of our friends haunt me. "She won't," Steffan argues, even though we both know it's futile.

"Every time we think we have this killer's agenda figured out, their MO changes. First, it was people who were acquaintances of all of us, then it became older members of The Illicit, and now its full-fledged elders and members. Your dad. Now my sister. Lois, who was Walter's lover. None of it makes sense." I shake my head in frustration.

Steffan's jaw clenches, and his eyes stare at nothing, yet somehow see everything. I know he's going over every death we've seen in the past nine months. An entire year of college that has been spent constantly chasing a killer, when it should have been spent partying, preparing pledges, and studying at the library.

"I refuse to lose to this psychopath," he mutters, and I can't help but grin. Of course he does.

"What do we know about Van Doren?"

"He's still in the wind," I remind him.

Another colossal mistake that was made. Van Doren needs to die. At first I was hesitant, thinking his exile was enough. I had wanted to spare Bailee some pain and heartbreak by letting her brother get away. I loved her, and even though they were estranged, I didn't want to hurt her. Then the ball happened, and I lost the woman I thought I would spend forever with. I gave her my tie. The same one they found wrapped around her neck, and listed as the cause of death. My chest squeezes remembering the coldness of her skin, and the way her eyes were open, screaming for me.

"Soren is working on it. I let him keep that little pet project. We should hear from him soon," he divulges.

My brow quirks. "He left Taylor alone with you?"

Steffan scoffs, "He knows she's safe with us." He sighs and runs a hand through his hair, "She's pretty torn up about Lois still, though. I let Kali stay with her while we are working on getting Chanda back. Your sister left an impression on Taylor. I don't want to scare her."

I lower my head to hide the small smile on my lips, a smile that has no business being there. Still, I like that she is close to my sister. I like that she is here, even when I shouldn't. She's their girl. Soren has made it very clear what Taylor means to them, and I have no intentions of ruining their relationship. Then I remember the sweet way she has been checking on me, the slight blush on her cheeks when I smile at her, and the way her pretty lips parted when my fingers accidentally skimmed over the skin on her arm. It shouldn't mean anything, but it does. Even when I know I don't stand a chance, and when I remember that the girl who could be considered my fiancée, died only a few months ago, none of it seems to matter when Taylor is around.

My eyes go to my best friend, and I swear I see a ghost of understanding in his eyes. He gets it. He already shares the love of his life with his brother. Their love is already complicated. I should not be thinking of ways to make her mine, too.

"Fuck," Steffan mutters, holding out his phone. "It's Soren."

"Answer it," I choke out the words, feeling as if my breath is frozen in my lungs. Everything stops while I listen to their clipped conversation.

"Okay," Steffan answers, his eyes moving to me. "Have Succo meet you."

Silence.

"I'm not surprised." He sighs and runs his hand over his forehead. "Do not tell them anything." The phone disconnects a second later. Steffan's hand lands on my shoulder and squeezes.

"They found her. She's alive. Succo is taking her to the hospital."

I feel the blood rushing through my ears, my pulse picking up again. I suck in air while he gives my shoulder a slap. "We should head out. I'm going to get the girls."

I nod, thankful he's giving me the minute I need to rub the wetness from my eyes and calm my racing heart. I need to let the emotion from the past few hours exit my body, and pull the mask of The Illicit back into place. Breathing through my nose, and exhaling through my parted lips, I push down the man who cares about his family, about his sister, about his friends. I hold on to it, suffocate it, trap it in the little box labeled feelings deep within my soul. There is no room in my life to have anyone, or anything, that can be used as leverage. Whoever this killer is, they already know too much.

"You should button up your shirt at least." A voice pulls my attention to the door. Kali stands there with her arms crossed, her leg popped while she stares at me. The usual sassiness in her voice is dialed down, but the same mischievousness still flickers in her eyes. Eyes that appear to be judging me right now. I feel a flicker of awareness travel through my body when she steps into the room, her long red hair swinging against the blue Thorn University T-shirt she wears. I watch as she moves in front of me, her hands reaching out to fix the buttons I had undone earlier. This feels wrong, having her stand so close in front of me, but I can't make myself push her away either. She's Taylor's friend.

"Ready?" Steffan's voice pulls me from my thoughts, and my eyes jump to the doorway. I didn't even hear him approach. Steffan is looking at his phone, so it's not his gaze I get trapped in. It's hers. Taylor's dark eyes ensnare mine. I swear I see a flash of disappointment in them, but it's quickly replaced with a small smile. Kali finally backs away from me, and goes to grab her bestie's hand. I'm stuck, though, unable to move. What the hell just happened? I want to make sense of it, but nothing about it makes sense.

She isn't yours.

I have to remind myself over and over again. Sure, we've grown closer, and yes, I protect her like she's one of my closest friends, but I do it for Steffan, my best friend, who is completely in love with Taylor. She's off-limits. I need to remember that. There isn't a doubt in my mind Soren would feed me to Allison if I so much as touched Taylor in the wrong way. He's been lenient with the time I spend with her, but I think that's mostly because she pushes him to be. She is trying to make me happy again. To heal me after losing someone important to me. Because I'm grieving. That's all it means... right?

CHAPTER TWO

Taylor

I still can't wrap my head around what has happened. I glance again at my boyfriend, and fight the urge to jab him with my elbow. I feel like such a spoiled princess. It doesn't matter that I've been upset about losing Lois, and scared for my family. I still should have known about Chanda being taken. We aren't besties but I hold a lot of respect for her. Chanda is fearless, and she isn't afraid to go after what she wants, and to protect her loved ones. My heart hurts thinking about what has happened while I've just been lying in bed. I love Steffan and Soren, but sometimes they leave me out of important things until they deem it safe for me to know. I should be there for them right now, and for Lee too.

Lee has become my friend. But, of course, the boys think I'm too delicate to handle everything that is going on. It's bullshit. I have been in the thick of bodies since day one at Thorn University. If I was going to tuck my tail and run, it would have happened already. There have been plenty of opportunities. Not that Soren would let me run. At this point, there is no escaping them, and I don't want to. I just want this nightmare to end.

"How is Chanda?" I ask Steffan again. After he got the phone call, he and Lee grabbed me from my room and quickly explained what was happening. We left the house shortly after and headed to the location where Soren and Jose are waiting with her. Steffan glances at me, and this time he must see how upset I really am. Instead of arguing, or lying, I see his shoulders fall, and he glances at Lee.

"She's a little roughed up, but alive."

"Soren found her?" I ask again. Before we left the house, my mind was still processing that Chanda had even been taken.

"He did," Steffan answers, while his hand grabs mine, "They found her at an abandoned warehouse."

"Within city limits?" Lee questions, and a look passes between them that I can't decipher.

"Why does it matter if it's within city limits?"

Kali scoffs, "Probably because that means the killer is close by. They didn't have time to stash her somewhere else."

"Kali." I nudge her, but all she does is roll her eyes. Steffan promised we could drop her off on our way out of town, as I didn't really want her walking. Not with some psycho after us, trying to pick us off one by one.

"They're probably already thinking about it," she explains and looks only half apologetic.

"My dad and the elders would only be interested in expanding resources, and the search area, if she wasn't within the city perimeter." Lee's voice is low and hollow.

My eyes meet his across the space of the car. A lifetime of sadness and emotion reflects in his eyes, and as always, I want to comfort him. I'm well aware of the rumors that follow us on campus. The voices are never as quiet as they think. Besides, I have a best friend named Kali who makes sure I indulge in every single wicked thing people are saying. So far, though, all I have been to Lee is a comfort. He's Steffan's best friend. He grew up alongside Soren. He's part of the Brotherhood and The Illicit. I can't imagine the pain he's been through. The way his green eyes bore into mine, like he wants me to read their secrets, makes my pulse race. It's crazy, and I'm not sure how to react or respond.

"They would have left her?"

His head nods, the dark chestnut locks falling into his eyes. My arms ache to hug him. I feel Steffan squeeze my hand, drawing my attention to him. He shakes his head, and his gaze flicks to Kali before coming back to me. He isn't stopping me from asking questions, or having the information I crave, but he is asking me to be mindful of the company I'm in. I still fight the urge to frown, though. Kali has been with me all year in this fucked up business. She knows more than she should already, and has never backstabbed me. I drop the subject and ignore the looks that Kali is shooting me. Her eyebrows lifted, asking silent questions that I'm answering with my own eyebrow dance. She knows I'll divulge everything to her later.

Within fifteen minutes, we're pulling up to the house that Kali and I share. I notice that there is a car outside, and when we pull up, four pledges I recognize get out. Steffan gets out, and they shake hands. Kali reaches over and gives me a hug before getting out. I watch as she waltzes past the brothers and into the house. I can only imagine how that interaction went since two of the guys are blushing, and Steffan is shaking his head when he gets back in.

"If she wasn't your friend," he mutters to me, a curse under his breath. I laugh lightly. My friend is a little headstrong, and has absolutely no filter. A few of the many reasons I love her to death.

We start driving again, and I realize it looks like we're heading out of town. I glance from Steffan to Lee, but neither of them feel the need to fill in the blanks for me right now. Alpha men are so irritating. The car rounds a curve and pulls off onto a dirt road. I glance out of the window and notice a closed-down bar that I didn't know existed. The parking lot is practically empty, except for two cars and a blacked-out van. Steffan gets out first and holds the door open for me. Slowly, I step out, feeling chills run down my arms. The vast darkness and shadows make the place feel eerily unsettling. As if sensing my hesitation, Steffan places his hand firmly on my back while he leads me toward the front door. Lee beats us to it and holds it open for us to pass through. The hallway is dark, illuminated only by green Exit signs, and a light coming from a room further down. I'm sandwiched between Steffan at my front and Lee at my back as we make our way toward the glowing fluorescent light. Shuffling feet and quiet voices float toward us the closer we get.

Steffan saunters into the room, taking my hand in his, and pulling me behind him. My eyes land first on Soren, and I feel the pressure in my chest lessen immediately. He's safe, and there isn't blood anywhere on him. His ice-blue eyes hold mine, confirming he's alright, and promising heat for later.

"Lee!" Chanda's voice pulls our attention.

I can't help the small gasp that leaves my lips. Chanda looks like she battled the devil and survived. Her tan skin is mottled with bruises, a thick cut edges her lips, and another decorates the corner of her eye. She's holding an ice pack against her head, and I assume she was hit there as well. Lee rushes to his sister and gingerly hugs her around the shoulders, keeping an awkward distance as Jose keeps Chanda on his lap with an arm around her waist.

A hint of a smile pulls at my lips, but I quickly push it away. It's not the time to smile, yet I can't help but be happy for Chanda. I knew there was sexual tension between the two, but their body language suggests there's more to it. The way both men embrace her makes my eyes sting with tears.

"What happened?" Lee asks, while his lips place a tender kiss on her head.

When Chanda pulls back, her eyes are glossy with tears. My heart squeezes seeing this strong woman so completely terrified and broken.

"Did he..."

"No." She shakes her head, her teeth sinking into her bottom lip. "No, not that."

"Tell me," Lee urges, bending down onto his knees, their eyes communicating in a silent battle.

"Jose." Her voice cracks.

"Leave, Scab!" Lee grabs for his hands, but they tighten on Chanda's hips. Her hand flies down to stop them both from fighting.

"No!" she gasps, her tears falling freely down her face. "No, I want him to stay."

Jose's eyes hauntingly meet hers, and it takes everything in me to stifle the sob that is threatening to escape from my chest.

"What do you want from me, Vixen?" His voice is like gravel.

Chanda moves from his lap, her body swaying slightly from the motion. Her hands pull both men to their feet. I watch as she positions them so Lee is standing in front of Jose, who looks lost and deeply hurt by the action.

"They only let me"—Chanda swallows tightly, and I notice for the first time the deep red marks marring her neck—"I only got to live so I could deliver a message."

She turns her back to us, her hand shakes as it reaches for the zipper of her black dress. Somehow I know what I'm about to see before it actually happens. The material falls away, the sticky, crackling noise of fabric peeling from blood echoes in the room. The animalistic yell that comes from Jose sends shivers down my spine. Lee turns to grab him before he can charge at Chanda. My own hands come up to the deep, red gashes across her back. The letters form the warning. A note. A message.

BLOOD.

CHAPTER THREE

Soren

My little mouse could barely sleep. Only after she took my brother and me into her body, and we wore her out, could she finally relax enough to close her eyes. She feels everything, my little mouse. Her heart hurts for Chanda and what she had to endure. I know she feels a sense of guilt, even though it is far from her fault that any of this has happened. It's not something I understand, but I will hold her anyway while she cries, and when she rages at the injustice of it all. Somewhere along the way she befriended Lee's sister, and her ache for her is deep. She has repeatedly attempted to heal Lee, too, a fact that has not gone unnoticed. I don't know how I feel about it, but I don't think I'd be able to deny her anything. Taylor's heart is too big, and it's all-encompassing.

Steffan is the last to untangle himself from her soft, now pliant, limbs. He dresses quietly while I take a quick smoke by the window, careful to blow the blue-gray smoke out into the chilled air. It is already the middle of April. There is one more month of school left, which means the time for preparing the pledges is almost over. Once Steffan is dressed in some sweatpants and a sweatshirt, we make our way down the stairs and into the game room. I close the door and lock it, before pulling out my phone and bringing up the live feed from the bedroom where we left Taylor. I place the phone on the mantel, within reach.

"Is she aware you watch her that possessively?" Lee mutters, but there is a slight slur to his words, probably due to the copious amounts of alcohol he has imbibed since we brought his sister back. He managed to help get her into his room, but we all know that by now she is in Succo's room. The poor guy's face has been hard as granite since we left the old Dug Out Bar. His body practically vibrated from having to hold himself back from putting his arms around his woman.

"What does it matter to you, Concord?" I keep my gaze focused on Taylor's sleeping form, baiting him into answering. I might kill him if he answers wrong.

Lee shakes his head and throws back more of the liquor in his tumbler. The room grows quiet except for our collective breathing.

"We've been playing defense for too long. The killer has become too bold. Lois, and now this with Chanda," Steffan finally speaks. My eyes glance at my brother, acknowledging him before falling back to my phone.

"So what is our plan, oh great one?"

"Chanda said they." Steffan keeps his eyes on Lee, who manages to nod and confirm the statement.

"She said it was definitely two people. The person who knocked her out was larger than the person who was in the room with her, who did the—" His hand gestures to his back, and the poor guy's face pales slightly.

"Carved her back like a fucking jack-o'-lantern?" I supply for him. His face whips to me, and the fury in his eyes is real.

"Soren," Steffan snaps, but I can't help laughing slightly.

"I'm making sure he's focusing. There's less than half a bottle of that vodka left."

"You're not helping," my brother groans, throwing his head back and running his hands over his face.

"Says you," I scoff and grab my phone off the mantel. I take a seat off to the side and prop the screen up with my knee. He wants to be a whiny bitch, then he can deal with not seeing our girl.

"Blood. Why carve that? What does that even mean?" Lee spins the liquor around in his glass. "We've been operating under the assumption that this person is random, or that they're after the power of The Illicit. Are we sure that is what is happening?"

"You think they aren't after The Illicit as a whole?" Steffan asks, and Lee's shoulders shrug.

"I thought it was revenge from the Van Dorens. We spilled Bryce's blood, he owes blood. Then we thought Dupree was seeking his inheritance and place in the Brotherhood. But Alex Dupree is dead, killed by his own blood, actually," I state, and they both turn to look at me. "If we can make sense of the killings, and who the victims have been, maybe we can understand the blood relation."

"We would have to start at the beginning." Steffan nods thoughtfully.

"That's a huge undertaking." Lee sighs and falls back in his seat.

"Let's not forget, dear brother, that we have four weeks until the pledges need to be ready. With Father gone, the elders are breathing heavily down our backs. If we're to achieve our goal, we need this initiation to be flawless. And we have yet to capture that fuck, Van Doren. Taking a walk down memory lane right now is going to require more than us, and more than the time we three have to give," I remind them.

Silence fills the room again. Time is not on our side for this one. We have eight months' worth of mystery and death to unravel, and now a new game to play.

"Do you think he was involved with what happened to Chanda?" Steffan asks Lee, who only manages to shake his head thoughtfully.

"I don't think he's smart enough to be the mastermind, but maybe he is helping another way. We need him. We need answers. Then he needs to die, and become acquainted with Allison again," Lee grits out before slamming his glass back.

For the first time, I'm actually impressed by Lee's idea and attitude. Usually he just follows whatever Steffan wants, and it's like having two of my brother in the room. This change is almost exciting.

"The girls could help," I suggest, the words slowly spilling from my tongue. I know it's not going to be a popular opinion, and honestly I'd rather be stabbed in the dick than have Taylor anywhere near the images of the killings again, but they might be more useful than us. Chanda was taken by them. Right now her memories are clouded by adrenaline, but in time, things may come back to her once her nervous system starts to recognize that she is safe.

"Are you out of your mind?" Steffan's eyes find mine and harden. I get it, I do. I hate to think of doing that to our little mouse. He has to admit, though, that she is more resilient than we give her credit for. She sees, and knows, even what we try to hide from her. It's part of the reason I fell for her. Those meek, innocent eyes are just a front for the devilishly smart angel hiding underneath.

"It's not like we couldn't use the help. Plus, they both already know what has been happening. It might even be cathartic for Chanda," I throw out as a last-ditch effort. It earns a chuckle from Lee, even as his eyes stay dark and glazed over.

"Might as well ask." Lee shrugs. "At this point, what can it hurt? It's not like Succo is going to let Chanda leave here anytime soon anyway."

"Oh good, you know now." I fake sigh, and make myself more comfortable in my chair.

"I was there, too—" Lee's eyes narrow. "Wait, how long have you known?"

"Probably since they started boning. I warned him, but he didn't listen. That, or your sister's pus—"

"Do not"—Lee jumps from his chair, swaying slightly, his finger pointed at my chest—"finish that sentence if you want to live, Carmichael."

My eyebrows jump, and I slide my favorite knife from my pocket. I flick it open and see Lee's eyes jump down to it. It happened quickly, and I'm sure Steffan didn't notice it, but I did. "If you want to keep both of your kidneys, I suggest you sit back down and never threaten me again, Lee."

Our eyes stay locked in a showdown that neither of us want to lose. I shift in my seat, and Lee moves over to the fireplace. His hands rest against the mantel, his back to us. I glance at Steffan, but he's watching the screen on my phone. The bed is empty. My heart lurches until I hear the click of the lock echo in the room, and the doorknob turns before swinging open.

Taylor is dressed in my T-shirt, her legs encased in a pair of Steffan's jogging pants. She looks sleepy, ruffled, and delicious. My little mouse has no idea that she has earned the attention of three hungry gazes. Her warm, amber eyes meet mine, and her chin lifts in defiance, making me instantly hard again. "You were listening, little mouse."

She nods slowly, her eyes narrowing with determination. "I'm helping. This psycho-fuck needs to be caught. And then I want you to make his death painful."

Yeah. We're all hard for her now.

CHAPTER FOUR

Taylor

Blood. So much blood. It's all I can see when I close my eyes. My heart breaks for Chanda and the pain she was put through. She's at least still alive, unlike Lois, unlike Ava, unlike all the others who have been brutally murdered in some psycho's need to prove something, the meaning of which none of us know.

I push myself harder, but no matter how hard I run, I can't outrun the visions and racing thoughts. I feel guilty even when I have no reason to. I just want to pull all my friends and loved ones into a bubble to keep us safe. My eyes squeeze shut while sweat runs like a river down the sides of my face, tracing my hairline. My feet pound against the asphalt of the track as my heart bounces in my ribcage. My lungs struggle to breathe in the crisp air while my body purges itself of the stress it's been under. *We're going to figure this out. It can't go on that much longer. It's been...*Half a year? Almost the entire school year. Yet we're nowhere close to figuring this out. *But we will.* I have to remain positive. I have to maintain some sense of hope. Faith. Undeniable and unshakable faith that we *will* get through this, and figure out who is connected to all of us, and holds so much vengeance. I need to find the inner peace I had and clung to, before I was swept away in this life by the men with whom I am so undeniably in love.

The one person I thought had plotted these murders is dead. Alex gave all the signs he knew what was happening at Thorn University before he was taken care of by Walter. My only other suspected person has been Bryce. Bryce has his reasons for issues with The Illicit, but I don't have any connection to him—other than as a pawn, or tool, against the twins. And I can't shake the feeling I am closer to these evil events than the guys believe I am. I feel it in my core. The same way I know I love Steffan and Soren. I know these killings have more to do with me.

Speaking of Steffan and Soren, how long can I be with both of them? How long until they believe maybe I am the issue, and don't want to keep this going between us. Worse, there's been a push and pull between Lee and me. At first, it was us merely finding comfort in one another. He was with me when I found the heart in my bed, and he found his girlfriend's murdered body in his bed. Our trauma keeps pulling us together. I keep seeking him out as a source of comfort that is different from the two boyfriends I already have. If Soren knew how I felt, I don't think he would respond well. Soren and Lee aren't exactly each other's favorite people. He's already made it clear he will only share me with his brother. I'm not sure how Steffan feels, but I know Lee is his best friend. Me bonding with Lee would only lead to trouble. I need to cut it off before either of us makes a choice that will hurt everyone. If we were to cross the line...I could lose them all.

We've already been blurring the line. Lingering eye contact. Hugs that last longer than acceptable to most people. Finding ways to have skin-on-skin contact. Little touches that somehow feel intimate and heated. I'm perfectly fine until we touch, but once we do electricity runs through me, heat pools at my core, and heart palpitations begin every time his arms encircle my body. His strong arms are so firm and hold me against him so tightly, yet so tenderly. When his long fingers brush against my hair to cup the back of my head, a tingling sensation always spreads from my neck down my spine. My mind feels betrayed that my body acts this way, and my heart screams at me to figure out what I'm doing. It feels instinctual to be with Lee, just like it was to be with Steffan and Soren. I'm already in a relationship with two men. Not to mention one is extremely possessive, and possibly unstable. They both adore and love me. I feel cherished and desired, yet here I am longing for the touch of their best friend. Their fraternity brother. I don't deserve the hearts of Steffan and Soren, but I want them. I want to be loved and owned by all of them.

Tears blend with sweat as I push my legs to their limits. The world around me is crumbling, and my very life is in danger. Meanwhile , I'm in turmoil over Lee Concord. I'm a horrible person. The pain in my chest is beginning to become too much. Stumbling to a halt, I bend over, placing my palms against my clammy knees. I heave and struggle for oxygen. Salty drops of sweat have my eyes stinging and watering. Everything begins crashing like waves at the forefront of my mind. Chanda being taken and mutilated. Lois, sweet dear soul *Lois,* so harshly ripped from us. My first roommate butchered. Alex, my ex-boyfriend, although a psycho, was murdered by his grandfather. So many deaths...I went from a small-town, wholesome girl, to losing my virginity to a stranger, and to sleeping with him and his twin. I don't even recognize who I've become through all this madness. A year of pure wickedness mixed with chaos. I feel shame, but no regret. The only guilt I have is my lack of regret because I wasn't raised this way—this goes against all of my upbringing, and years of what's been ingrained within me.

The pressure in my chest is constricting my oxygen supply. My emotions are bubbling and have nowhere else to go but out. I open my mouth and allow the scream to rip from my throat. I feel myself screaming, but all I hear is a ringing in my ears. I should care more. I should have done more.

My body finally registers pain as my knees hit the ground. Everything slowly eases to a calmness as my breathing regulates. The grain of the asphalt burns my palms, but at least it's snapping me out of my head. I allow my body to roll over onto my back and stare up into the blue sky. My chest rises and falls out of sync with my racing heartbeat. I'm not a runner. I have no idea why I thought this was a good idea. I couldn't take the pent up energy in my body any longer.

Thankfully, I have the Blue Rose High School track all to myself today. It was nice to push my body to exhaustion and scream my heart out in privacy. The relief of just being able to get all that out and not have an audience. I promised the guys I'd bring someone with me, but I *needed* this. Everyone needs to have their space, and to be alone sometimes to have a breakdown.

Ssssshhh. Sssshh.

A soft static noise comes through the sound system instantly pulling me from my internal struggle, and disturbing my sense of peace. I rise up to a sitting position and look around. Nobody is here. *Sssssh. Sssssh. Pop!* I cover my ears as the static hisses and pops. Quickly I get to my feet and look around as I slowly lower my hands from my ears to my sides.

Nobody.

There's nobody else here. Shivers spread up my spine as I try to peer up at the announcer's box, but all I see is darkness.

"Heeeel-heeelp. Hel-help..."

Straining my ears, I listen to a hoarse voice beg for help through the intercom system. I don't stop to think. I force my exhausted legs to get me to the bleachers. Metal bangs beneath my feet as I hurry up. I pause and listen. "*Hel...Help. Me...*"

Instinct has my body frozen on the stairs. It could be a trap. I know I was here alone. I ease my phone out of my pocket before I go any further. I glance at my contacts, my finger hovering over the names. Soren would lose his mind if he discovered I deliberately put myself in danger. Steffan is the more rational one, so I call him.

"Hello, Little Mouse," he purrs into the phone.

"Steffan..."

"What's wrong?"

"I'm at the high school track. I know I shouldn't have come alone, but I think someone is hurt. A raspy voice is coming from the sound system, and they're asking for help."

"Where are you? Shit. Taylor, do not go towards the voice. This could be a trap to lure you up there. Get back to your car—no wait—there could be someone there if they think you'll run. I need you to get to the center of the field where you'll be in a wide open space. Nobody can corner you or sneak up on you. Stay there. I'm on my way."

"Okay. Thank you."

I hear him barking orders to someone else and I assume it's Soren, or Lee. Even Jose would be great right now. "Don't hang up. You're going to remain on the phone with me until I can see you're safe."

My feet pound against the metal bleachers as I hurry back down. Adrenaline floods my veins and my instinct to flee catches up with me. Goosebumps decorate my skin, and I feel the flushed feeling of being watched on my back. My name being called catches my attention. I stop. What was that? The voice spoke again, but I couldn't hear over the metal rattling, or the frantic sound of fear in their voice.

"Taylor...Help. Me."

"Steffan," I cry into my phone. "They said my name."

"Get. To. The. Center. Now! Run, Taylor! Run, baby!" I can hear Steffan's car engine rev. He is barely maintaining his cool. I do as he says and hurry down the rest of the bleachers. The sun is beginning to set. Thankfully, Steffan will be here before it's dark. I shouldn't have come alone. This was so stupid of me. All I wanted was some privacy, a moment to myself.

I reach the center of the football field that the track circles. "*Help me... Taylor... Heeelp.*" The lights switch on which makes trying to see the announcer's box extremely difficult. In fact, I can't see anything from the top of the bleachers and on. I hear the sound of a motor, and my shoulders relax. But it's wrong. It sounds too rough, not the smooth purr of Steffan's luxury sedan. I look behind to see a row of school buses parked on the other side of the wire fence. The one in the center has its lights on.

"*Help me... Heeelp...*"

The bus slightly sways as it begins moving forward. As it comes closer, I narrow my eyes, trying to see who is driving. Someone is wearing a mask like Soren's from Halloween. It's a neon skeleton mask. The bus engine roars as it picks up speed. It barrels into the fence. "No," I say into the phone, panic lacing through my heart.

"Taylor! Taylor!" I hear Steffan's voice commanding an answer. "What's going on?"

"Do you know where Soren is?" I manage to breathe out, my eyes locked on the school bus.

"He's on his way. What's that noise?"

"Are you sure he isn't already here?" Maybe that is Soren, and he is bringing the bus to help. Doubtful. My mind wants the best scenario for this one.

"Impossible. Why? What the fuck is happening? What's that noise?"

The bus reverses only to charge forward again, this time knocking down the fence. I scream as I turn to run. I bring the phone back to my ear, "Steffan?"

"I'm here! I'm on the road leading to the high school." He voice is tight, I can tell he's holding in his violence and worry for me.

"Someone is driving a bus wearing Soren's mask. They just plowed through the fence like this is some action movie! I'm running away! Please hurry! Please find me!" The phone slips from my hand and I take off toward the only other opening on the field, praying my legs don't give out, and that I can outrun whoever is hellbent on killing me today.

CHAPTER FIVE

Steffan

Beep. Beep. Beep. Call ended. I drop the phone in my seat, my hands tight knuckling over the steering wheel. My foot pushes further on the gas. I'm determined to get there and I don't care about any speeding laws at this point. I swear if anyone has hurt her, I will make them suffer beyond their worst imaginings. This is the longest drive of my life, my teeth draw blood from my tongue, my jaw is clenched so hard. If anything happens to Taylor, I will never be the same. She has fixed my life in so many ways while giving me the grace to also be myself. She knows the world I live in, about the throne I must rule, and she loves me anyway. She loves my brother, even though he's the definition of a psychopath. I suspect she's close to loving my best friend too, and surprisingly, that doesn't bother me. It feels complete in some way. I need to be there. I need her safe, to rescue her.

My tires screech as I finally turn into the school parking lot. I shove the gear shift into park and jump out of the car, not bothering to shut off the engine. I have to find Taylor. My eyes scan the surroundings, but I don't see her. The lights are on around the track, and all I hear is static from the sound system. The fence is down, and the bus is idling in the center of the field. Tire tracks now marr the usual pure, green turf.

There's a piercing screech, and suddenly, the sound of an old record begins. A haunting voice crooning, "You Are My Sunshine," fills the night air. This psycho keeps making everything more bizarre. The record screeches and plays again. Then it does it again. It's repeating a verse on a loop. I stop to listen. *"But if you leave me, to love another, you'll regret it all someday..."*

This time the record continues playing. They have my attention and they know it. They're watching me. Awareness fills my senses and I scan the area as I slowly approach the football field. I haven't loved and left anyone. Taylor's ex is already dead. Who stole this fucker's sunshine?

A light flashes in the grass and I jog over to it. Taylor's cell phone lights up with Soren's name on the caller ID. I pocket her phone just as the song begins again. By the time my boots touch the asphalt track, I've looked all over and I can't find our girl. Panic squeezes my heart in a death grip knowing that Lee, Jose, and Soren aren't here yet, but should be showing up soon. I can't wait any longer. I run up the bleachers toward the announcer's box knowing this could be a trap, but I have to get to Taylor. I know someone is in there because they were rewinding the verse. In my peripheral vision, I see headlights. Thank fuck! When I turn my head I see Lee's truck coming in at full speed.

Once I reach the door, I lean my head to the side to try and listen for anyone on the other side, but the music is too loud. Going to have to risk it. I throw the door open, and the chemical smell that hits my nose has me gagging. There's a haze of smoke, but I can make out a figure heading straight for me. Before I can react, I'm shoved to the side, and something cold and sharp is against my neck. I try to fight them off, but they're wearing a mask, and I'm breathing this shit in. My eyes are watering, and whatever they just injected into me already has my body weakening. I'm fucked and I don't see Taylor.

"Steffan!" It's Lee, they're here.

My head rolls to the side, my muscles are unable to move, and I can feel my consciousness starting to fade. My eyes land on a body on the ground holding the microphone. Is that Taylor? *Taylor. Taylor!* I'm screaming her name in my head, but the words aren't coming out of my mouth. I can't move my mouth. *Taylor!*

"Fucker!" It's Lee again. Two blurry forms fight in front of me. I should move. I need to get out of their way. What's all this smoke? Hey...I know this song...my parents used to sing it...they'd play it at some of The Illicit galas back when I was little... *Please... don't... take... my... sunshine...*

CHAPTER SIX

Taylor

I hear a commotion, but I don't dare move. The bus floor is dirty, and the seats smell sweaty, but so far, I've been safe. I ran as hard as I could, trying to remain in the shadows to get to the line of buses. I figured they wouldn't expect me to go that way. I lost my phone and I have no idea where the guys are, or how close they are to getting here. The creepiest version of "You Are My Sunshine" has been playing nonstop. I'm ninety percent certain this is some form of torture, or part of their mind games.

"Enough fuckers! Get your asses out here! You got your little spotlights and fucked up music playing, now let's have at it. Step into the arena with me!"

Soren.

I ease up to my knees to peek through the window, but I can't see. I'm going to have to go to the front of the bus. The rough floor scrapes my skin as I crawl toward the front. I remain on the floor and only rise up enough until I can see, trying to remain in the shadows. There's Soren standing in the middle of the football field. My beautiful psychopath. He bangs his fist against the bus as he challenges our attacker to come face him. Of course he wants this over, and wants whoever is doing this to face him. He spreads his arms out wide and laughs into the night sky. "Let's play, motherfucker!"

I'm about to run to him, to stop him from being too reckless, when movement on the bleachers catches my attention. It's Lee carrying Steffan! Soren notices as well because he takes off in a run. I ease out of the bus, my heart pounding in my chest, but I won't run. No matter how badly I want to run and check on them, we can't all be running. I have to keep my guard up.

Staying in the shadows, I try to keep my footsteps light as I make my way toward the guys. A motorcycle noise comes from my left. I gasp as I turn in time to see a person dressed in black, wearing a helmet, just on the other side of the fence. They rev their engine and lift their black, gloved hand to slowly wave at me. Then they drive off. That was them. In my gut, I know that has been the killer this whole time. But why didn't they shoot me, cut me, or do anything ? They taunted me. That slow creepy wave will haunt my dreams tonight.

I take off in a sprint toward the guys. By the time I reach them, Lee and Soren have Steffan on the ground and are on the phone with The Illicit's personal doctor. Steffan is rambling, and his eyes are glassy.

"Taylor...she's on the ground..."

I fall to his side and take his hand, which is cold and clammy. “I’m here. I’m right here.”

Soren narrows his eyes at me, so I knew I’d be in trouble, but there’s also fear there. Lee turns to Soren and tells him, “There might’ve been someone else in there.”

Steffan’s twin grumbles, “I’ll go check. Yell at me if he gets worse. Doc is on the way.” He points his finger at me and my cheeks turn pink. “You stay fucking put.”

Lee shakes his head, his eyes sympathetic when they fall on me. “He’s scared. He doesn’t have to be such an asshole about it, but he turned white as a sheet when he saw Steffan.”

“I know,” I whisper, and I do. I’m in my own panic right now looking at Steffan, knowing he came here to rescue me, and now he’s hurt. I think back to the wave the driver of the motorcycle gave me. I wasn’t their intended target. I feel it. They wanted him. Or Soren. Or Lee.

Steffan groans and shivers. “I know the song. Gala. Ah...ah...” His body locks up and only his eyes are moving. His entire body is stiff. I frantically touch him not knowing what to do, but needing to feel him and make sure his heart is still beating. It is, but it’s terrifying how immobile he has become. Tears spring to my eyes and I hold in a sob until his body relaxes.

“L-Lee... Lee...”

Lee takes his other hand. “I’m here, buddy. I’m here.”

“You’re...a-always there. You, and my little mouse. I love you.”

Before either of us can comment, the doctor arrives. Lee kept the needle, and some of the fluid they injected into him is still in it. A few of The Illicit members arrive as well. Steffan is an important member, so him being attacked, and possibly killed, is a high alert. I caused this...

Steffan could suffer permanent damage, and may still die, because of me.

"Where is Soren?" a woman in a designer, fitted suit demands.

Lee stands to answer her. "Up there. He went to check if anybody else is here."

"You let him go alone? Brother Concord, do you not—never mind." She turns to a few men in black suits. "Get up there and help Brother Carmichael."

They turn to go just as Soren appears at the top of the bleachers carrying a limp body with long brown hair. He reaches us and sets her down next to Steffan. The doctor checks her pulse and says, "It's very faint." He begins to examine her, but the lady clears her throat.

"Dr. Arshad, you are here for Brother Carmichael."

The doctor grunts and returns his focus to Steffan. "Well, she's as good as dead anyway. I'll have to take this back to the lab, but if I had to guess, both of them were injected with the same stuff. Only young Mr. Carmichael here didn't get a full dose. I'll get him stable, and then let's take him to the facility."

"Why in the hell was Steffan out here without protection? Backup? He needs his men."

Soren crosses his arms. "We were on our way."

"No. He needs people with him at all times. And you as well. Don't you get it? You're the future of The Illicit. God help us." Her cold blue eyes turn to me. "Why do I feel like you're the reason Steffan broke protocol? Did his little mouse get into trouble so he came running?"

I flinch under her gaze. The weight of her words are already piercing my heart. Soren takes a step closer to her, "Watch it."

She smirks at him before her face turns to stone as she commands, "Get your rodent infestation under control."

With a snap of her fingers, the men lift Steffan onto a gurney, and place him in the back of a black van with the doctor. Lee wraps his arms around me as we stand, pulling my body into his side. Soren snarls but doesn't speak out. I say a silent prayer for Steffan as they disappear out of the parking lot.

"Who do you think she is?" I ask as I look down at the girl who has silently passed away.

Soren raises his hand, it's bloody. "Shit. I didn't even notice before. It must've come from her." He gently rolls her onto her side. The entire back of her shirt is soaked in blood. Soren lifts her shirt hesitantly.

FOR is carved into her back, deeper, rougher looking by the way her skin is flayed, but identical to Chanda's wound. Chanda had BLOOD carved onto her back, and this girl has FOR carved into her skin.

"She was alive and begging me for help. She knew my name." This is too much. I start to hyperventilate, my lungs are unable to grasp air. "That was her in the announcer's box. That was her! She begged me! What if they were carving her up like a piece of meat while I was standing down here. She probably saw me just standing there!"

Lee pulls me tighter to him. I cry into his shirt. "Why is this happening? Everyone around me keeps suffering. Now look at Steffan. I can't lose him, too. I can't."

"But you don't recognize her?" Soren asks.

I look back down at the lifeless body. "No. But she knew my name."

"Maybe they told her to say it. Sick fucks." He tries to reassure me, but the damage is done. Either way she is dead, and I feel like an accomplice. I stood by and did nothing. But if Steffan dies, I'll feel like the murderer. I brought him to his death.

CHAPTER SEVEN

Lee

Steffan isn't in a good place, and all I can think about is him. My best friend. My brother. The one person who really knows me, more than my family, more than my sister. His injuries were life threatening. He could have died. Whatever was injected into him almost stopped his heart.

Hearts being cut out.

Snakes inside bodies.

Skin carved into angel wings.

Messages carved into skin.

None of it makes sense and it is all too much. I run my hands through my hair and feel the weight of the past year settle on my shoulders. The Illicit is fucked if we don't find out who is targeting us, and why. Well, more of the why than I already assume. My eyes glance over to *their* little mouse.

Taylor is wrapped in Soren's arms, finally sleeping, even if it's not peaceful. Her forehead is scrunched, and her fingers still flinch in her sleep, as if the whole day is playing on repeat in her dreams. I watch as Soren squeezes her tighter, holding her body to his chest as if he's afraid someone will snatch her, and it will be her body we find next. We've come too close. My sister. Taylor. Steffan. Bailee. As always, the guilt I feel over her death hits me in the gut. I haven't thought about her in a few days and now her memory is plaguing the back of my mind, reminding me of what is important. I can hear Taylor's frantic pleas for Steffan to live, and still see the way she crumbled into the grass. We need to find who the sick psycho is that continues to hunt us.

"I'm tired of doing this." The words fall out of my mouth, and I chase them back with a swallow of the liquor I'm nursing in my glass.

Soren's eyes snap to mine, and I see the irritation in them. I also see the streak of nothingness that he often toes the line with. Steffan and I are dangerous. Deadly. But there is always a little something darker, and more disturbing, that lives inside Soren. "What the hell is that supposed to mean?"

I hold his blank gaze before dropping my eyes down to Taylor. Her lips part softly in sleep while she breathes in and out. At least she's fucking breathing. "I'm done living on the defense. All we've been doing this year is going around in circles, too scared to get out of line with The Illicit, and covering our tracks."

"And what do you suggest we do? You know my brother will kill both of us if we step out of line with the Brotherhood."

My eyes turn glacial. "Right now, he isn't doing much of anything since he almost died."

Soren's face shudders, and the monster he hides fights to the surface, "Like I said, what are you suggesting?" he grits out through clenched teeth, loud enough to be frightening but not loud enough to wake Taylor.

"I'm done with playing defense. It's all we've been doing. With Alex Dupree, with Bryce, and with this killer. We've been running around covering our asses, and the person is always one step ahead of us. I want answers. I'm ready to bring the fight to them, and fuck what The Illicit say." I manage to keep my voice, calm, firm, but I hear the deadly undertone. We can't run anymore. If my father, or the other members, have anything to say about it, then they can come here. Only we both know they won't while we're being hunted. Rhett Carmichael dying was a big fuck you, and trouble for The Illicit. Now with Steffan fighting for his life, the members have to be shitting their pants. I know all the brothers at the house are.

Soren doesn't answer for the longest time. His hand runs through Taylor's hair, and his mind takes him far away from reality, his eyes zoned out and his face blank. The ice continues to melt in my drink, and I keep my gaze focused on Taylor. On the feelings circling in my chest whenever I think about her. The twins weren't the only ones who panicked today when we got the phone call. It felt like my worst nightmare all over again, only worse. If she was hurt, I would hurt, but Steffan and Soren would also be in unimaginable pain.

"I need to speak to Succo. I have an idea, but it will require him and his skill set. This could mean a war if The Illicit feel we are trying to overpower them by going against their wishes. I couldn't give a fuck less about what they think, but diplomacy," Soren shrugs slightly, and I think of Steffan. He would be the one to remind us of all the backlash we could face. "Watch her for me." Soren moves gently, letting Taylor lie flat on the couch while he stands up. I manage to nod, but I can't keep my gaze off her. He leaves the room, his cell phone already up to his ear.

Even in sleep, she is a stunning woman. This is the other thing I am sick of fighting. I know I'm attracted to Taylor. On some level I think she's attracted to me, too. It's a war I fight within myself, knowing she's my best friend's girl and also knowing that she is the one person who has kept me going, and kept me focused, the past few months. Every time I felt like giving up, she was there to make things better. She healed me in a way my sister and my friends couldn't. I can't ignore that pull I feel toward her. I used to think Steffan and Soren were in way over their heads, and wonder how their hearts could possibly be okay with sharing her. Now that I know her, and her sweetness, her angelic soul, it makes sense. They both want any piece of her she is willing to give.

Taylor lays oblivious to my thoughts and the dirty scenarios my imagination cooks up. All the ways I'd like to twist her up and make her beg for me, while in the next second I would share her with my best friend and his brother. As long as I got to have her. As long as, on some level, she was also mine, and she screams my name to heaven when I make her come hard. I picture her dark brown eyes hooded with desire while I pump into her over and over again.

"Lee." Her breathy voice pulls me from my fantasy, and the reality of our situation crashes around me again. I move from my chair until I'm kneeling in front of her on the couch.

"Hey, beautiful," I whisper and run my fingers along her cheek to her jaw. It's the most intimate touch I've given Taylor, and I blame it on the thoughts still running rampant in my head, the voices begging me to slide into her and make her mine as well.

Taylor's eyes widen and her cheeks turn pink, but she lets me continue my path over her other cheek. Her body softens, and I can't help the way my heart jumps in my chest from just being this close to her. "Is everyone mad at me?"

I freeze at her question, my teeth setting on edge. "Why the fuck would anyone be mad at you? Did someone say something?"

A small sob catches in her throat, and her hands wrap around my wrist. "It's my fault Steffan got hurt. That the poor girl died because of me. You all are always telling me to be careful, and to stay near, but I left campus. It's all my fault."

I shake my head, refusing to let her believe the bullshit the killer wants her to feel. "No. No, Taylor, you are not responsible for any of this. You should be able to have space. Steffan and Soren understand that you need space. You've been through hell. No one could have predicted this."

"But the only reason they came there was to save me." Her body shakes with her tears and sobs.

I shift so I'm on my knees as close to her as possible, and drape my arms around her. "Of course they did.

They love you. Nothing would stop them from coming to find you if you were hurt, and trust me, Taylor, if anything had happened to you, they wouldn't survive. The only reason we are all pushing through and staying in this fight is because of you, beautiful girl."

"I want them all gone, Lee." Her voice breaks, and I see a hint of madness in her gaze. "Bryce. The killer. I want them all gone, dead, buried, sinking at the bottom of the lake with Allison. I don't care how it gets done, but it needs to happen. I can't keep losing people I love."

Her words are like a hot wire straight to the darkest part of my soul. I get it. I was just saying the same thing to Soren. We've all been building to this moment, and I'm ready to go to war. I know Soren, and probably Jose, will be in. He hasn't been right since almost losing Chanda. We're all getting desperate. Deep in my heart, I know Steffan would feel the same. He may be the voice of reason for all of us, but is also swift to hand out justice and punishment. With his back to a corner, I know he'd fight back with us. And our backs are to a fucking corner.

My fingers reach out and touch her chin, tilting her head up so she's forced to look right at me. Taylor has seen my worst days. She has seen when I couldn't stand, or move, and all I did was curl in on myself and shut the world away. I want to be the one to give her the peace she craves. "We're going to end it. I promise. I'm done running, and the guys are, too."

Her nostrils flare, and there is a dark triumph in her gaze. She doesn't move from my grip, and before I realize it, I've moved closer to her. I see her throat swallow quickly, and the rise and fall of her chest deepens. "I can't hold back with you anymore."

Taylor sucks in a breath, but again she doesn't move out of my grasp. It's like she wants it just as badly as I do, for us to finally cross this line that we've been drawing around each other. I should keep her firmly in the friend box, but there is nothing that feels right about that. The twins might kill me for touching her, but I think I will die on my own if I don't at least try.

I touch my lips to hers, hesitant at first, just a brush against the pink pillows, but that's all it takes. She tastes like all my darkest fantasies, and she isn't pushing me away, or screaming for help. My lips drop back to hers, devouring her mouth, sucking and biting, in case I never have an opportunity again to feel this. I don't even realize it at first, but she's kissing me back. One of her hands in my hair and the other gripping my wrist. I need to stop, to take a breath before the line is completely gone, but fuck it. I don't care anymore.

Taylor pulls back first, breathing hard and swiping her tongue across her lip. Her eyes find mine, and I see the questions in them. Questions I don't have answers to, except this wasn't a mistake, and yes, I want to do it again. Preferably without an audience the first time, but I'm open to the guys being around for the second or third time. "That was—"

"Perfect," I tell her, feeling the growl in my chest. "You taste exactly as I thought you would. Just like heaven."

Her pupils dilate, and her cheeks flush pink again, "I don't know what this means. I'm just causing more problems."

"Don't," I tell her and shake my head. "You didn't do anything. I don't regret anything about your lips being on mine."

She's about to say more, maybe argue with me, I'm not sure, because Soren walks back in the room. I'm sure his spidey senses were just tingling. His eyes widen a fraction at my proximity to Taylor, but it melts away when he sees that she is awake.

"How are you feeling, little mouse?"

Taylor watches him closely, but I see the love and devotion on her face. "I'm sorry. I'm so sorry. I just want him to be okay."

"You have nothing to be sorry for." Soren walks over and takes her face in his hands, kissing her forehead, inhaling her scent. "We would move heaven and earth to keep you safe. Steff is going to be okay. He's under observation, and as soon as he wakes up, we'll go see him."

"Promise?" Her bottom lip wobbles and tears make her eyes shine.

"Yeah, I do," Soren answers and releases her. "Lee and I need to go take care of something first. Jose and Chanda are coming over so you can sleep. When I get back, we'll go see him."

Taylor instantly relaxes at his words, and his promises. I raise my own brow at him, wondering what the hell the plan is. I don't get a chance to ask before Chanda waltzes into the room like she owns the place. Jose is not far behind, and I can see the murderous look in his eyes. It hasn't eased up any since my sister's back was carved.

"I thought you said you had information?" he says and glances between us.

"I do," Soren assures him before moving over to the sidebar and flipping a hidden compartment. The top flies off, and he grabs the gun and loads a clip into it. "Taylor will fill you in on what happened. We'll be right back."

Taylor's eyes jump between us, and I can see her wheels spinning. If possible, her cheeks flush even redder. "Soren," she calls his name, and his gaze instantly jumps to her. He cocks his head, and his brow rises.

"Be safe, and come back. I want both of you to come back."

My stomach clenches. She probably thinks Soren is on his way to get rid of me as well, and I praise her. I follow Soren out of the house, and we both get into his car. It sits there idling while he stares into space. "What did you do?"

I shake my head. "Nothing she didn't want me to do. And if she tells you differently, I will help you sever my head from my body."

His frosty blue gaze stays focused outside of the car, but his hands grip the steering wheel. "I would never leave any part of you for them to find, Concord. Just remember that. You're playing a dangerous game."

"I'd expect no less."

CHAPTER EIGHT

Soren

The tip I got on Bryce better be accurate. If this fucker lives one more day, I won't be able to take it. I need to feel him take his last breath. I need to listen while he screams, and begs me for another chance. I won't be able to close my eyes until I see Allison take him whole and drag his limp body to the bottom of the lake. Everything in my heart, soul, body tells me that Bryce had something to do with what happened today. I don't believe he did it himself because, let's be honest, he isn't that bright, but he knows who did it. My senses are telling me he was there.

Taylor could have been killed. My brother almost died. I can't lose either of them, and they sure as fuck can't leave me here alone while they stay together for eternity. I won't allow it. And since I'm not ready to leave everything behind, I need to fix things. I can't have my girl, my world, blaming herself for us being too soft.

Lee was fucking right when he said we need to take action.

I glance at Lee and see the determined look in his eyes. It's been months since I've seen this fight in him, as if he also found the will to live. I know it's because of Taylor. I could tell the minute I walked into the room that something had shifted between them. I hope he was fucking careful, too, because my little mouse is jumpy, and she tends to take on more than she can be responsible for. I'm not exactly sure what it is Lee is hoping to get from my girl, and I sure as hell hope he isn't thinking he wants her the way I do. Just like with my brother, no one will ever want her as much as I do. I will share with my twin, because the obsessive part of my brain tells me he looks like me. It's essentially like Taylor gets two of me. Lee is another story. That and because I've never been super fond of him. I tolerate him. He's a friend, and a brother, but that's where my loyalty ends. And if he's fucking with Taylor because he isn't in the right head space, I will end him. Steffan can find a new best friend.

"What is our plan here?" Lee asks, his eyes finally snapping over to me.

"I got a tip on Van Doren," I grit through my teeth. "That rat has made it too far without feeling our wrath."

Lee grunts and nods his head. "There can't be any mistakes this time. If we end him, it needs to be quick and quiet. Until The Illicit is free of corruption, and this killer has been caught, we can't let them know."

"I thought you were all in, balls to the wall. We're ending these fuckers one after the other. The Illicit can burn in flames for all I care."

"Steffan will care," Lee reminds me. "Don't get me wrong, I'm all for ending the fucker. It's been a long time coming. I'm just saying we keep it between us while we start battling back. If The Illicit are in trouble, I don't want them trying to hang us to save themselves."

Damn it. I hate when he makes sense. I get it. I do. I'm just ready to burn the world down to keep Taylor safe. "Fine. We will do it your way for now."

"Great." Lee smirks sarcastically. "So tell me where we're going now."

I share the info I got with Lee, and tell him about my gut feeling that Bryce is part of what has been happening. We take a quiet road out of town, and I grab the gas can from my trunk, filling it up. The road is empty, and the cameras in this store have been under our control for years. Eventually, we head back toward campus. I watch Lee's reaction as I drive us to the outer edge near the stadium, toward the one building you would think Bryce would be too smart to be in.

"The football house?" Lee's eyebrows jump in surprise and confusion. "He's an idiot."

I nod in agreement. "And they're all dead men walking for hiding him. We've given enough chances to these meatheads."

I get out of the car, and Lee follows after a few seconds. I'm already gone, though, moving stealthily through the trees, staying in the shadows of the property, trailing a happy little stream of gasoline behind me. All the while I can hear noise from inside and lots of male laughter. They aren't going to know what hit them. I round back to the front and stand next to Lee.

He glances at me. "You're going to start the house on fire?"

I smirk and say, "No," before tossing him the lighter, "You are."

Lee flips the silver lighter around in his hands, sliding it between his fingers. "Then what?"

"We'll grab Bryce when he bolts. We both know he'll run to save himself. He always does."

"What about the others?" Lee questions, and I see him teetering on the line.

"They've been hiding him, and they know the consequences." I shrug before delivering the final bullet. "He hurt our girl. My brother's life is hanging in the balance, and they all knew they were hiding him."

He doesn't think twice. The lighter drops from his fingers and soon the trail of gasoline takes on a bluish glow before bursting into flames. I slap Lee on the shoulder, and we wait. It doesn't take long before the flames eat at the bushes and lick their way over the old wood of the house. Smoke billows into the air, and a split second later, the fire alarms are going off. The house is absolute chaos, but I keep my eyes on the exits. Sure enough, while everyone is managing to get out the doors, and searching for their other brothers, one lone figure appears on the roof and is scurrying toward the fire escape. Just like a rat.

Lee and I bolt to the end of the ladder. Lee wrestles Bryce down to his knees, and my arms slip around his neck. I tighten my grip and squeeze. Bryce fights, grabbing and clawing at my arm, trying to land punches to my side. I take it all, his death looming over him is what keeps me going. Once Bryce passes the fuck out, Lee and I manage to get him into the trunk of the car.

As we drive away, the fire truck finally appears. They are too late, though. The house is already engulfed in flames, the black smoke rising into the night sky. I wish I had my camera to capture the moment.

I drive past our house and think of my little mouse. I hope she's sleeping and waiting for me. We head onto the dirt road past the house, through the grove of trees, until finally we come to the edge of the water where our other favorite girl is waiting. Lee and I hop out of the car and move to the back. I grab my gun, prepared for Bryce to leap out. Lee pops the trunk, and we see Bryce cowering.

"I didn't mean to!" he pleads, but his words are falling on deaf ears. I want answers and then he needs to go.

Lee grabs Bryce and throws him to the ground. Bryce lands on his bad leg, and it's enough to keep him down, howling in pain. "Fuck you, Carmichael!" he spits and yells, getting so worked up his face is turning red.

I lean down so I'm eye level with him, keeping my gun pointed at him the entire time. "You messed with the Brotherhood, Van Doren. Steffan is in the hospital, and worse, you messed with my girl, and that is something I can't forgive."

"I didn't do shit." He laughs. It's the wild look in his eyes that has me losing my cool.

I crack the butt of the gun across his face, loving the blood that sprays out of his mouth when his head turns. "Guess you lost some of your brain when you lost some of your leg. There is no getting out of it this time, Bryce. You're done. Your family is through. You made enemies out of the wrong people. If Steffan was here, he might cut you a deal, but not me. I have no conscience, and losing you doesn't tear me up inside."

"The Illicit will have something to say about it." He smirks as if he thinks that will buy him more time. I can feel the ripple in the water coming our way. Bryce's life is limited.

"The Illicit can suck my dick." I laugh in his face and point to the black, inky water. "They'll never find you anyway."

Bryce's face turns white when he glances at the water. "What do you want?"

"Tell us who did it," Lee jumps in. I hear the impatience in his voice, but I'll let him have this.

"You should be careful, Concord. The true killer is always closer to you than you think." Bryce smirks even as his body shakes on the ground.

Lee snaps and is on his knees with Bryce's shirt in his hands. "Tell us who you fucking helped!"

Bryce's maniacal laugh floats in the air, and I see the gleam in his eyes. He's made peace with his impending death. "Ask your father."

Lee loses his shit. His hand is around Bryce's neck, his body pinning him to the ground while his fist lands punches all over Bryce's face. I give him a minute to let his aggression out. I get it, we're all hurting right now and pissed off.

"Enough," I finally growl, and Lee gets back up to his feet and takes a walk. I get down close to Bryce and level my gun at him again. "Any last words?"

"None of you are safe," he heaves around his words, and blood pours from his lips.

"We're The Illicit. We're never safe," I remind him. With one last glance at my fallen brother, I stand, and with a pull of the trigger, Bryce no longer exists. Lee walks back over, and together we drag his body to the edge of the water.

"Snack time, baby girl," I whisper to her, knowing she is right there. She is always waiting. Allison's massive jaw breaks through the water, and she clamps down on Bryce's limp body, wrestling him from the sand and dragging him under.

"We didn't learn shit," Lee huffs and runs his hands over his face.

"Sure we did," I tell him before grabbing a cigarette from my pocket and lighting it up. "The killer is after The Illicit. Your family seems to be a prime target, but so is mine. Bryce knew his life was over either way. My guess is if we didn't do it, the killer would have. They weren't close."

We both watch while the water swirls with blood and the gnashing of teeth on bone filters into the air. I feel lighter, that at least one loose end has finally been tied up. Whoever this fucker is doesn't have a lackey anymore. They're on their own, and now it's our time to hunt. My phone vibrates in my pocket, and I grab it. Lee glances at me.

"Steffan's awake."

CHAPTER NINE

Delta Pi Theta Mansion

Taylor

With the guys gone, I can't shake the shame that I feel in my stomach. I feel dirty knowing I betrayed the two men who swear they love me. I didn't know I was going to kiss Lee. I've been attracted to him, he did save my life, and on an emotional level, we connected. When I woke up he was there, his green eyes held so much warmth in them for me. When he touched my skin, the burning need in my blood surfaced. The kiss didn't feel wrong, but I don't know what to do with it. I've sworn my love and devotion to Soren and Steffan.

My head is a mess right now, and after what happened today, I have nowhere to go. I really can't leave anymore, or I risk putting all our lives in danger. I don't dare call Kali either. She'll hear the shake in my voice and be on her way here. I need her to stay away for now. I'm too scared she'll be next.

I shift off the couch and move to the fireplace, watching the flames dance. I remember my father often preaching about sins and fire. If only he could see me now. In the distance, sirens have been speeding by all night. I gave up caring at this point, and deep inside, I know it's because of my guys. My guys. Soren is mine, and I don't know what to make of Lee. I need Steffan. I need him to talk to us, and to make everything alright again. If anyone would know how to handle this calmly, it would be him. Would he hate his best friend, though? They both have been very clear about no one else touching me, or coming near me. "I'm such a mess," I whisper to the fire and run my hands down my face.

"A beautiful disaster," Soren's voice answers from the door, and I spin toward him. My eyes take in every inch of his clothing, his shoes covered in grass, dirt on his pants, and specks of dark liquid reflecting on his deep blue shirt. The cords in his neck stand out when he swallows while I check every inch of him. The red specks on his neck confirm what I already knew would happen.

"You made us safe?"

Soren steps further into the room, each movement predatory as he keeps his eyes on mine. My heart races in my chest the closer he gets. I keep waiting for his lips to turn mocking, or his face to show disgust at what I did. I get none of that, and soon he's in front of me, taking my hand in his.

"Steff is awake," he tells me, his head tipped slightly.

I feel like I can't breathe. I'm happy, relieved, ashamed, and I still blame myself for Steffan almost dying. A sob tears from my throat, and it borders on a scream. "Can I see him?"

Soren steps into me and wraps his arms around my body. "We're all going to go see him. I need to shower first." He pulls back and keeps his hand around mine, leading me out of the room and toward his bedroom.

"Soren," I say his name lightly, but he doesn't answer. His hand just holds mine tighter. I have so many questions, and so many things to say, but it feels as if he's avoiding the conversation.

In his room Soren locks the door behind us and pushes me into the bathroom with him. I watch while he starts the shower and begins stripping out of his clothes. The more layers he takes off, the more blood and gore I begin to see. "Who?"

Soren shakes his head, "As much as I like talking about murder and death to you while I'm naked, this is one of those times we do have to wait for my brother."

I can't help the small smile that tugs on my lips. I move to give him space while he showers, but Soren has other ideas. His hands are pulling at my T-shirt and tugging it off over my head before I can exhale.

"Strip it all off, little mouse," he commands, and my body moves to please him. I need this, to feel a connection to him right now. Soren always seems to read this about me. I reach for my leggings and slide them down my legs. My bra and panties follow, and soon I'm naked and flushed in front of him. Soren groans low in his throat. His hands move into my hair before he's kissing me. His body slams into mine, pushing me into the wall while he devours my mouth. My hands are everywhere on him, pulling him closer, scraping down his back, trying to fuse myself to him as close as possible. I can feel the steady rhythm of his heartbeat against mine. It reminds me that I'm alive. We're here. And this man who is invading my senses is keeping me safe. He wants me.

"Soren." His name falls off my lips and is dripping with need. My core aches, and all I want is to be filled by him.

Soren knows what I need, and I see the glint in his eye warning me I'm going to get it with his special brand. His hands move over my body and grip the back of my legs. I'm lifted off the ground, and I wrap myself around him, holding tight when he walks us into the shower. The hot spray hits my skin, and I jump in his arms, his hard length brushing against my slick wetness. I push my breasts into his chest, and he groans. The sound is husky and desperate.

My back hits the wall, and Soren braces one hand against the wall, the other locked tightly under my ass. His hips shift, and he slides inside with one quick thrust. My head flies back, my mouth opening while I moan his name. Soren's thrusts are ruthless, burying himself inside me before sliding almost all the way out. He thrusts hard, punishing, claiming. He shows no mercy, mad with lust until I'm screaming for him, my nails digging into his skin so hard I'm leaving marks. Soren's lips find mine again, and he bites hard on my bottom lip. My eyes fly open, and I see the sinister look in his gaze.

"Are you mine still, little mouse?"

"Yes," I gasp against his lips.

"Damn right," he groans, panting between words, "You'll always be mine, little mouse. No matter who you kiss, you'll always be mine."

"Yours." The word falls from my lips right as my climax hits. My body convulses around his, pulling him in deeper, my legs squeezing at his sides.

"Fuck yes, little mouse," Soren says loudly, his eyes shutter closed. His hips snap against mine again and again before his head falls back, and he's biting his own lip with his release. I feel the hot spurts of cum paint my insides. We're both breathless from our release, and my body sags into his, my legs feeling boneless.

"Let's get washed up so we can go see Steffan," Soren says. His words remind me of what is really important. My fear, my worries, are not what matters. Our life, our family is important. Finding out who is trying to ruin us, ruin our happiness, is all that I should be worried about.

Soren washes my hair and my body before his. When we're done in the shower, we dry off and change quickly in order to get to where they are keeping Steffan. The minute my feet touch the entryway floor I can feel Lee's eyes on us, taking in our matching wet hair. Guilt slithers inside my belly, and I force myself to look past him. I can't look at him right now, and fear to see anything that resembles sadness. Soren squeezes my hand. I need to stay focused. We all need Steffan.

CHAPTER TEN

Blue Rose Hospital

Steffan

My head feels fuzzy, and there are dull aches all over my body. Where's my little mouse? Taylor! She's in danger! *Taylor! Taylor! I'm coming! Please be okay. I'm coming, baby. I'm going to save you...*

"Steffan."

Yes! I'm here, my little mouse. I won't let anyone hurt you.

"Steffan? Can you hear me?"

I hear your sweet voice.

"Open your eyes. Please." Her voice cracks. "Open them for me." So much emotion is behind her words. I need to see her, but my eyelids are heavy. "Are you sure he's awake?"

"He's awake. There's movement behind his eyelids, and his charts are improving." I don't recognize the male voice.

Slowly, light comes to me as my eyes open. It's all hazy and out of focus. There's movement, but I can't quite make out the shapes yet. My tongue weighs down in my mouth. I can't get it to move to form words.

"Water. Get him some water," the stranger's voice demands.

I'm so damn tired. The only relief is Taylor is well. She's here and sounds good. Admittedly a bit frantic, and I hate she's worrying over me. Doesn't she know it would take Satan himself to drag me away from her?

A dark blur of color comes toward me, and then I feel plastic against my cracked lips. The water feels heavenly. Cool and soothing. Tears come to my dry eyes. As I blink them away, everything finally shifts into focus. I'm in a hospital. There's Dr. Arshad, a member of The Illicit. A few other committee members stand off to the side. Soren—who looks ready to murder everyone. Lee. And my little mouse.

"Mouse," I croak.

Taylor bursts into tears and comes to wrap her arms around me. Dr. Arshad asks me a few questions about how I feel and what I remember. *I feel like shit and remember every fucking thing*. He explains they're still not sure what all I was injected with, but they're going to run a few tests. Worst part, my ass is stuck here for a few days. He makes his exit and then does me a solid by telling The Illicit committee members that I need my rest. They all shuffle away and soon the tension in the air starts to dissipate. My arms tighten around my girl, and I watch as Soren and Lee wince at her pain. I want to hurt the person who did this to me, to us, just so she doesn't have to go through this again. What I am not prepared for is the slew of self-deprecation that comes from her mouth.

Taylor spends a good thirty minutes crying and apologizing. Lee, Soren, and Succo try to help me reassure her that it's not her fault. My arms tighten every time she tries to blame herself more. Taylor should be able to jog, and live a life, without someone trying to kill us. It takes all of us to make her feel even the slightest bit better. She stops crying, but I can see the agony deep in her eyes when she looks at me. It makes my stomach twist and my chest tighten. That look is almost worse than death. Eventually, my brother can't take it anymore and Soren offers to take her to get a drink from the vending machine. With them gone I have a moment to find out what they've learned.

Lee fills me in on what's been happening in the few hours I've been out. After listening to it all I can't help but stare at him. Once again he was there for me, like he always is. I know Lee's been hurting, and this has been the year from hell for him especially. Yet here he is, helping my brother, and looking after my girl, keeping up with The Illicit, and by my bedside. And he's burning with vengeance and blood lust. Although after what we've been through and seeing the toll it's taken on Taylor, I'm with them on this.

Unfortunately, I can't handle much more conversation. They give me more medicine to ease the pain. After a few minutes I feel my whole body relax so much that I'm not sure if I'm still on the bed, or floating above everyone. I close my eyes to relish the sweet relief.

My eyes flutter open, and there's Lee holding me like he did when we were on the football field.

"Lee." I can't help but smile as I look into his gorgeous green eyes. They're so big and such a vivid color, it's fucking hypnotic.

"Steffan." His voice is rough. "You scared the shit out of me, you dick."

I laugh and am surprised when it doesn't hurt. This medicine is some good shit. "Close call, but I'm harder to kill than that. Where is everyone?"

His face comes closer to mine. "Who?"

"Everyone else?" My eyes stare at his full lips. I bet they taste as sinful as they look.

"I don't know. I don't give a fuck about anyone else." His lips are a breath away from mine. My heart is beating against my ribs, and for the first time, I feel pain. Between my legs, my dick is throbbing, and I desperately need to get some friction.

"Lee." I swallow. "What are you doing?"

"What do you want me to be doing?"

"I don't know."

"Fucking liar. Didn't think you'd have such tiny balls, *president*."

Sexual frustration, deliriousness, who the hell knows why, but I grab his wrist and shove his hand between my legs. "Why don't you find out how tiny my balls are?"

He firmly grips me, and I can't help but buck further into him. My release comes long and hard.

"Somebody is having a nice dream." *Taylor?* My eyes fly open to see Taylor standing next to my bed.

I'm still in the hospital. Oh shit. I just had a wet dream about my best friend. What's gotten into me?

I could've died. That's always a risk with this life, The Illicit especially, but now that I almost did, it's sinking in. Right before I faded out, Lee was there holding me. *Lee.* My best friend for years. My *Delta Pi Theta* brother. We're both fucking legacies. I'm the new leader of The Illicit, and he's the only Conrad boy, so he's known as the prince. Our families are at the top of the ranks. Naturally I care about him. We are the future. We're going to rule...together? *Together, together?*

No. Yes. Together as best friends. Brothers. Lee has never once looked or acted as if he was interested in anything else. Before this year, he was the playboy of the house. We've grown up together, been naked in front of one another in gym, and walked in on each other fucking on more than one occasion. We've never come close to crossing any lines.

I can't ruin our friendship now. Plus, I love Taylor. But my feelings for Lee are more than lust. Have I always loved him, but been too blind to see? Pushed it to the back of my mind. Denied it for years. Taylor loves more than one person, so it's possible I could, too. There are enough problems circling us. I'm probably in shock and scared. My thoughts are running rampant. I love Lee, of course, but as family. Yes. I need to get back focused before I do end up with a toe tag.

Taylor comes back to my bed with a wet cloth. "Let me help you clean up." She pulls back the hospital gown with the wet cum stain. "What were you dreaming about?"

"I'm not sure." That's partly true. I'm not sure what was happening.

"When I was little, I heard a dream is a wish your heart makes."

"Nightmares, too?" I tease.

"I didn't ask about those. But yours clearly was not a nightmare." She finishes cleaning me up and grabs a new nightgown for me. "Maybe next time it doesn't have to be a dream."

My breath gets caught in my chest as she leans down and kisses my temple.

Maybe.

JOURNAL ENTRY

It's all finally happening. Finally. FINALLY!

Rhett Carmichael. Dead.

Walter Dupree. Destroyed. He's lost the love of his life plus his only heir.

Steffan Carmichael. Down. Weakened. Easy prey.

I'm saving the crown jewel.

Lee.

I need to toy with the Concords some more. What's going to hurt him most? Soon The Illicit will be dwindled down to nothing. Just like they left us. My family.

Taylor is the key. She has no clue how much she's helped me. Do I allow her to see it all unravel?

Or do I use her to pull the last string? The final thread that completely wrecks the Brotherhood...

CHAPTER ELEVEN

Concord Estate in Alabama

Lee

It's been two weeks, and Steffan has been moved to one of the safe houses. He has round the clock nurses and a physical therapist that comes every day. Guards, top-of-the-line security, the place is a fortress, yet I still don't feel comfortable leaving.

However, my father is demanding I come home to discuss Illicit business. I talked a big game with Soren, and I feel powerful when I'm with my brothers, but I shrink back into a little boy every time that son of a bitch calls me. The fact is, I still want his approval while at the same time, I hope I become nothing like the man he is. I look like my father in every way except my eyes. Those are my mother's. He hates that, complains that we have the eyes that can look into a person's soul. Maybe we do. Because I know when I look at him, I don't see a soul.

At one time, the Concords were the head family. Amir Concord has always seemed content to pull strings behind the scenes. Allow himself time for his shady side businesses and other forms of corruption. The Illicit and *Delta Pi Theta* crests have a snake, and Amir Concord is ever the snake. I don't trust him, and it's dangerous not to trust your own family.

My mother sits in the sunroom sipping a glass of wine. "Well, look what we have here. My son has returned. I was worried he'd forgotten me." Dove Concord is one of the most beautiful women in the world. She used to be so witty and fun, but the world has chipped away at her so much that all that remains is a cold shell. To be fair, she was younger than me when my father married her. I don't think they had a true love story, or if they were ever happy. My sister was born first, a daughter. And according to my father she was hardly useful as the first born. They did eventually have me, but I know they argue about it. I can remember when I was little and I would wake up, hearing my parents argue, glass break. Sometimes I wonder if things with Bailee were predestined to end horribly, because relationships in my family are disasters. Despite how my father makes me feel, or his less than desirable treatment of my mother, she is one of my favorite people.

"He could never." I smile down at her, reassuring her that my love is still there.

She smirks at me, and I see a glimmer in her green eyes of the woman she was before. "He better not."

I place an affectionate kiss on her forehead and feel her body relax. Her delicate, thin hands take mine and squeeze. "It's so miserable in this house with you and your sister gone. Too quiet. I'm so lonely."

"Why don't you go over to the tennis courts at The Illicit clubhouse?" It's basically a country club, but only for the elite of *our* society.

"Those banshees. Lee, darling, you know all those women are either shriveled evil hags, or sniveling child brides."

"Mother. Child brides sounds..."

"Twenty-year-old gold diggers then. The only one of the lot I can tolerate is Margot. But now that Rhett's dead, all she does is weep at home." There's no sympathy for her widowed friend. My mother doesn't mean to sound cruel, I'm sure. It's just she doesn't know what it's like to be married and actually love your husband. If my father died, she'd probably dance on his grave.

"You should go visit her."

"I want to, but I've not received *permission*." She says the last word with evident distaste.

"You're not here to see me. I'm sure you won't tell me why your father has sent for you. I'll simply be grateful you spared a minute for the woman who birthed you."

"Mother. Stop."

"I know I'm nothing more than an incubator and show pony. Promise me you'll never treat your wife as such." I nod, but she doesn't release my hand. A single brow raises, and she whispers, "Or... any significant other."

I narrow my eyes. "What do you mean by that?"

"Nothing. How's Steffan? I heard he was knocking at death's door."

Jerking my hand free, I tell her through pursed lips, "He's fine."

"Good thing death didn't answer. Life's short and fragile, my son. You should know that by now."

Don't I? It seems that living these days is like gambling on a wheel of Russian roulette. I'm not sure what all my mom's rambling is about, but I need to see my father.

"Where is dad?" I ask her, my fingers giving her shoulders a little squeeze.

Her eyes roll and she takes another drink of her wine, "His study. He has company though."

My brow raises, "Who?"

"The grandfather of The Illicit," She scoffs and takes another drink. "Go on and see them. Will you please stop by though this week for dinner maybe? I miss you. And bring your sister."

"Sure thing, Mom," I lean down and place a quick kiss on her cheek. "Love you."

"Love you too, baby," She waves me off and grabs a magazine to read as I walk away.

Sure enough my father is in his study just as my mom said. His voice carries into the hallway the closer I get to him. When I open the giant double mahogany doors, my eyes widen in surprise to find Walter Dupree sitting on the camel leather sofa, across from my father who is in his favorite navy suede upright chair. It resembles more of a medieval throne. Tacky. Presumptuous, very telling about the man who is sitting in it.

"Son," my father announces, his eyes narrowing as he looks at me, even though he pretends to smile.

"Father. Mr. Dupree." I greet them and take a seat on the smaller navy suede chair.

They go back to discussing business, my father pretending I'm not here, or that I don't know the business of The Illicit. He rambles a bit about The Illicit's financial standing, possible expansions, and other bullshit that is not accurate which only shows further how out of touch this current generation is. Walter must be thinking the same thing because he looks both bored, and also irritated, while listening to him.

"Now, Lee," my father turns to me, "you said they're leaving messages now?"

Dupree lights a cigar and narrows his eyes at my father. "Your daughter had a word carved on her back, did she not?"

My father grunts and takes a pull of his cigar, leaning back in his chair and acting like my sister is beneath him.

"'BLOOD," I jump in, answering Walter and my father, " and then another girl was found with 'FOR.' My guess is the next one will be blood, again. Blood for blood."

Dupree's graying eyebrows pull together. "That's a Concord phrase."

My father looks very displeased. "It is. The girl at the football field wasn't a coincidence. She's of Concord blood. Not closely related, but she is. Somebody is digging, and working on cutting our family tree down."

Dupree ponders for a moment and then says, "Blood for blood. Revenge. I would ask who have you crossed, Concord, but that's a list I don't have time for. Interesting that the message was put on the women of the bloodline?"

He scoffs. "Easier prey. Weaker than the men."

The original founder of the Brotherhood laughs at my father. "Steffan was on his deathbed. Your son-in-law is dead. But your daughter *lives*. You're a fool. Always have been. You underestimate women, and that will be your downfall."

He's right. My father's ego will certainly be his demise. Luckily, The Illicit won't end, but be improved, and stronger when the twins and I take over. I won't voice that thought out loud of course. Instead, I sit patiently taking in the information being exchanged as I idly twirl the family rings on my fingers. Dupree voices a thought I'd been wondering myself. "What secrets are you hiding, Concord?"

My father sputters. "You've miraculously risen from the dead, and now waltz in here demanding to know my skeletons in the closet? You can go fuck yourself. My family will continue to prosper because I made it that way, and not because some sniveling women think they can handle the amount of power it takes to run The Illicit."

Dupree is on his feet with a mini pistol pointed at my father's stunned expression. "Watch your tone with me. I made you. You have all of this *because* of me. And I can just as easily take it away."

"Where were you hiding that? My men searched you." My father's eyes bulge and the look of betrayal on his face is almost comical.

"This isn't my first day, son. I think I can manage to get a small weapon past your boys. Like I said, you underestimate people. If you think I'm not a threat because I'm an old man, you're more dimwitted than I originally thought. You're not going to make it to old age." He turns to me. "Get ready to take over. Your pops here isn't going to last much longer."

My father stands up and shouts, "How dare you turn your back on me! Come into my house and threaten me. Demanding answers. You fucking coward. You went into hiding and only came out now because that psychopath grandson of yours was on the loose!"

Dupree spins around and roundhouse kicks my father in the gut. He falls backward and lands back in his chair. "I was through with the bullshit and corruption. I wanted to finally get to live in peace. But I don't owe you an explanation, you ungrateful piece of shit."

Father reaches into his coat pocket, and I jump in front of Dupree. "Stop!"

"Move. I won't repeat myself." My father's eyes have a far away look in them, the thick purple vein in his forehead pulses with his racing blood. It's almost as if he can't believe he is being challenged, or that anyone would question him, let alone, Walter Dupree.

"Dad. You can't kill him." I hold up my hands, gesturing for peace.

"I'm Amir Concord. I can do whatever the fuck I want."

I pull out my gun and aim it at him. “And I’m Lee Concord.”

“Nice to see you don’t just suck balls, but you actually have a pair. I was beginning to worry, son.” He scoffs, and right then and there, I decide I hate him a little more.

Before I can charge, Dupree pulls me back. “Don’t fall for it. He’s baiting you. Keep your emotions in check.” He speaks louder and asks my father, “You’re agitated because you’re guilty. What are you hiding? You know something. Did you bring this upon the Brotherhood?”

“Get the fuck out of my house before I shoot you both.”

He’s made up his mind. We’re not going to get anywhere. And even though I want to believe he wouldn’t kill his heir, my father now knows who stands with me, and that soon no one will stand with him and The Illicit. I nudge Dupree, and we walk backward toward the door. If my father really wanted us dead, he would’ve already sent his guards after us. As I’m walking Dupree to the door, my mother comes rushing toward me.

“Goodbye, Mom.”

Her arms wrap around me, and I sigh into her hair. Then she speaks, and my blood turns cold. “He framed the Van Dorens. That was *our* money.”

“What?” I can’t breathe.

“There’s something else you should know. Your father has another child out there. I don’t know he—”

Boom.

My mother’s jolts in my arms. Our eyes meet and her’s go wide. Her lips part in a silent cry.

No!

Everything stops. *Mom! Mom! No, no, no, no.* I hold her to me and help her ease to the ground. A circle of red blooms on her chest growing larger with every beat of her heart, her life essence seeping out. I glance behind me and I see my father is standing at the balcony with his gun still pointed in our direction.

"Mom, Mom, Mom," I plead. I can't take another loss. I can't. She was good. *Good.* She didn't deserve to be married to him. Dupree is yelling for help, and trying to assist me, but we both know it's futile. I know what is happening and I can't stop it. I can't stop her bleeding. My hands cover her chest, my fingers turning red and sticky.

"Lee. Be happy. Whatever that means, or costs, be happy. Life's...too...short not to...be." She gives me a little smile as her eyes begin to close. "I love you and Chanda. You two...were my happiness."

"Mom. *Mom!*" I stare down as the only person who ever truly loved and cared about me takes her last few breaths, her fingers sliding away from my sleeve. She dies in my arms. The worst part—she looks at peace. She was but a beautiful bird kept in a cage. "You're free now."

I whisper into her hair, my body hunched over her protectively. It's time for me to be free as well. I take my phone out and call Soren. I stare at my father as I speak to my brother. "It's war."

CHAPTER TWELVE

Taylor

I'm stretched out on the floor in Steffan's room. I've read the same page in my textbook at least five times, and still none of the words are registering. I'm consumed with worry for Lee. He has become distant since his mother's funeral. Rightfully so. He spends hours planning strategies with Dupree, Soren and Succo. Then he checks on Steffan and me. His sister is back in lockdown since now we have to worry about the killer *and* Amir Concord. Unless they're the same person. I'm not entirely convinced Amir isn't the killer, or working with this person. He would know all the intimate details the killer seems to know. Maybe this explains Chanda being captured, but only injured and then freed. Everyone else has been left for dead.

Chanda doesn't think it's her father. She said she would've known, despite never seeing her captors s. She does believe he would have another child. He had several mistresses over the years.

Instead of closing in on answers, it seems we keep unraveling more mysteries. Who is the secret child? Just because there's an illegitimate child running around shouldn't make them a suspect. There has to be more.

"What was she about to tell Lee that was so serious his father shot her?" I ask Steffan, who has been improving tremendously.

"Little mouse." His voice is gentle, but firm.

I look up from my homework that's spread out across the floor. "Yes?"

Steffan pats the side of the bed where he's lying. Physical therapy wore him out today, so he recently woke up from a nap, and as soon as his eyes opened, I've been bombarding him with all my racing thoughts. When I stand my legs are stiff and my back aches. *How long have I been down here pretending to do homework...*

I sit and smile down at him. I'm so grateful that my prayers were answered, and Steffan is still here with me. I'd love nothing more than for all of us to have days of carefree happiness. Threats on our lives have been nonstop. Countless deaths weighing us down. That's what scares me the most about falling in love with the boys who are a part of The Illicit. Will our lives always be like this?

Steffan takes my hand and gives it a gentle squeeze. "I know you're worried about Lee. I am, too. But I'm a little jealous right now."

The playful gleam in his eyes is making me blush. "Why?"

"Because you're worrying about Lee, and not the danger my dick is in." When my jaw drops, Steffan starts laughing. My eyes ease down to see the tent he is pitching. We haven't had sex since... Well, honestly, I haven't even touched him because I've been so scared. He almost died. I don't want to accidentally set back his healing process.

Steffan senses my nervousness. His hand releases mine to graze my cheek. "I'm okay."

"You almost died because of—"

"No."

"What if I hurt you...again?"

"You didn't." His tone is exasperated. I flinch because I know he's tired of saying it. "You never have. And you won't." Seeing that I'm still not convinced, he tells me, "How about you go over to that chair and show me how wet your pussy is for me."

I guess he figures he might as well get a show if I'm not going to touch him. When he smiles and waggles his eyebrows, I roll my eyes. "Cocky much? How do you know it even is?"

Of course, I am wet for him. I'm always eager and ready when it comes to the Carmichael twins. He doesn't need to know that, though.

"Then get it wet for me." His voice is husky and demanding. "Make yourself come for me. I want to watch you spread that sweet pussy and play with it until that chair is soaking."

That shouldn't be too hard since his filthy words already have me about to explode. Excitement rushes through me. I walk over and with my back to him, I pull my top over my head. Steffan releases a low hum of approval. Painfully slow movements, I strip down my pants before sitting. I place my heels on the seat of the chair and spread my legs wide for him. Cool air tickles against the overly sensitive skin.

"Wider, little mouse."

I follow his command. My heart is painful against my ribs. This feels so taboo. I love it but at the same time I'm vulnerable and exposed. Seeing his eyes heat and become hooded, I also feel powerful. Sexy. Seductive. I'm a bundle of conflicting emotions. Pushing forward, I reach my fingers down.

Steffan stops me again. "Wet your fingers first."

Even though I feel as though there's a river down there, I stick two in my mouth. He licks his lips and then he demands, "Push them further back." My eyes widen because I feel like I'm gagging myself. "Wet your fingers like you would my dick."

Closing my eyes, I push the two fingers back and pretend like I'm sucking his dick. I wish I was. Maybe after this, I will.

"That's it. God you look so hot right now. Your pussy glistening. Sucking your fingers. My little church mouse is quite the naughty slut. Okay, baby. Show me how you pleasure yourself."

I bring my saliva-coated fingers between my legs. Slowly I spread a coating over my already wet lips. Steffan watches me with intense focus. He nods his head, giving me encouragement. That's the main difference between Steffan and Soren. Steffan always offers compliments and words of encouragement. Soren simply stares you down and dares you to keep going. He challenges me. Both push me to come out of my shell and comfort zone. I love both of them for it. I crave the push and pull between the twins. The hot and cold. Yet both love me equally, and I know they'd do anything to protect me.

Thinking about them has me getting even more worked up. I moan and close my eyes as I throw my head back.

"Yes. We need to get that handled." What? Steffan speaking to someone other than me brings me completely back to the present. "No. Yes. Now's good." Is he seriously taking a phone call? Steffan turns the phone away from his lips. "Don't stop until I tell you." Then he goes back to his call.

The nerve. I've gone this far, and I need my orgasm, so I continue. Steffan hisses through his teeth as I insert two fingers inside of me. He ends the call and says to me, "Deeper. I want to see your knuckles disappear."

Knock. Knock.

Oh for crying out loud! I'm never going to orgasm. I look around the chair for something to cover myself. "Shit! Steffan!"

"Don't you dare get up." He tells me in a tone you'd use on a child. It's gentle but firm. It's easy for him to say, I'm *naked.* I expect him to tell the person on the other side of the door to come back, but instead he says, "Come in, Lee."

Lee! I look at Steffan and sarcastically tell him, "Suuuure. Come on in." Then I hiss, "What are you doing?"

This is not good. He doesn't answer me, just leaves me wondering what he's thinking – or is he even thinking? Lee must wonder the same thing because his eyes widen as he looks between the two of us. He quickly slams the door shut and scratches the back of his neck. "Steffan, you said now's a good time." He clears his throat repeatedly and his voice quivers. "Did I misunderstand you?"

"Keep going, little mouse. Lee doesn't mind, do you?"

"What?" Lee sounds as shocked as I am. What if I mind? What's going on with him?

His face is completely calm, giving nothing away. His tone is even and confident. "Do you mind if Taylor gets off while we talk business?"

"Yeah. Yeah, I do, man." Lee, however, is unraveling.

Steffan chuckles. "I get it. I can't take my eyes off her, and I won't be able to focus until she comes."

"I can come back." Lee starts toward the door, but Steffan stops him.

"Wait. Before you go, I need to taste her. Wet your fingers, and bring me a sample."

Lee's chest rises and falls as he stares directly between my legs and then at Steffan. "She can bring her ass over there and sit on your face. What the fuck?"

"No. I still want to watch her. Now do it." My body trembles at the thought of Lee touching me there. I'm not sure what's really happening, but God, it's exciting.

Steffan finally cracks a little crooked smile. "Little mouse. Do you mind if Lee touches you? Does he have your permission?"

This is it. Before I was mad that he didn't ask, but now he has, and all the pressure is on me. I'm going to have to either admit I want it, or deny myself the pleasure. I've denied myself for too many years. Looking directly into Steffan's eyes, I speak. "I don't mind at all."

Lee's eyes bore into mine as he roughly slides my hand out of the way. He doesn't hold back. Two large fingers slide into me, and I can't stop myself from whimpering in pleasure. Two pumps, and then he pulls them out and walks over to Steffan.

"Did you smell her?" Steffan asks.

Then it clicks inside of me. Of course he's doing this. He knows. That's what all this is. He knows I've kissed Lee, and that I've been eyeing his best friend and fraternity brother. My thoughts immediately come to a screeching halt when Lee brings his fingers up to his nose, and I want to die of humiliation. He must lick his finger because Steffan snaps. "I didn't say you could have a taste."

Lee's voice has gone from shaky to confident and hungry. "I couldn't resist after I smelled how delicious she was . There's still some for you, and plenty more where that came from."

I about orgasm right there at the sight of Lee sliding his fingers between Steffan's lips. They stare into each other's eyes as Steffan sucks Lee's fingers the same way I did mine earlier. He pulls back and growls at Lee, "You want what's mine?"

"No." Well, that hurts. But then his voice turns guttural, and he confesses, "I want her *and* you."

"What the fuck is going on?" Soren roars. I didn't

even hear the door open. I was too entranced by the erotic sight before me.

"Taylor, get fucking dressed *now!*" his voice booms.

"Don't you move," Steffan demands. He stares at his twin. "You're free to join us, brother."

Soren is seething. He tilts his head and snarls at Steffan. "You're lucky you're already on bedrest."

Steffan scoffs. "Stop with the dramatics. Join us, or leave. I've gone long enough without."

"So you're what? Going to fuck anyone that comes in, and *share* what's ours? Are you high?"

Steffan's eyes turn ice cold. "Lee isn't anyone."

"He's not me. Is he my replacement? You two going to share Taylor now?" Steffan doesn't say anything, and Soren's pain is evident on his face. "You didn't even think about how I'd feel, brother? How would you like to walk in on me displaying our girl like that? Fuck this. Taylor, are you staying or going?"

All eyes are on me. To be fair, Steffan didn't ask me until later. He didn't allow me to cover myself. I'm not sure what's going on with him, but that doesn't excuse no communication before jumping into something like this. I stand and grab a throw blanket to wrap around myself. "I'm going, but by myself. I need to be alone."

I'm going to call Kali. I need a friend right now.

CHAPTER THIRTEEN

Soren

My feet sink in the mush as I get closer toward the banks of the water. I need to clear my head before I torch the whole mansion. All I see is red. The whooshing of the blood raging through my veins is deafening. The surge of anger is inflaming every fracture of my soul. It's white-hot, and can't be ignored or pushed down. It's bubbling out of me. I want bloodshed. Lee couldn't touch her. She's mine. Brother or not. Founding family or not. My knuckles are turning white, and my teeth are about to grind themselves to dust because I'm unable to contain my fury. If Steffan hadn't been there, I would've painted the walls with Lee's insides.

Lee.

That sneaky, worthless, sorry son of a bitch. I'd like to carve his pretty boy face up. He's worse than that prick Van Doren, and Alex. This whole time he's been waiting to make a move on *my* girl. I share her with my twin, my blood, my other half from the fucking womb. But I'm not going to share her with some pampered dumbass.

Fucking Lee.

First he tries to steal all of Steffan's attention from me. Now that motherfucker is moving in on Taylor. What the hell? The next question that plagues my mind is if Taylor wanted Lee. My girl hasn't had much experience with guys. Is she one of the many who can't resist Lee's charm and bullshit? What if she comes to me and tells me she wants him?

"FUCK!"

We don't have time for this. I need to keep my head in the game but the idea of Taylor not receiving what she wants... I'd murder for her. Killing is easy, though. Sharing is a very serious problem for me. I'd gladly give her Lee's body stiff and cold, turning a nice shade of blue. I don't want to lose her. She and Steffan keep me grounded, and focused. They're the only people I give a shit about, other than Allison.

I stop under the willow tree. The dampness from the ground is soaking through my pants, but screw it. I light a cigarette and stare out into the dark murky waters. Two yellow eyes break through the surface and blink at me.

I'd solve a lot of my problems by feeding him to Allison. He'd be a nice treat for her since he's all about clean and healthy eating. Then again, I think she's enjoyed some of the ones I've given her that still had drugs in their system... *Fucking junkie alligator*. Immediately, I feel regret. I can't talk about my girl like that.

"I'm sorry. I didn't mean it, baby," I tell her and take another drag from my cigarette.

"Apologizing to your invisible girlfriend?"

I about shit myself at the female voice at my side. A wave of anger courses through me again. I'm so upset that I didn't even pay attention to my surroundings. Nobody should be able to sneak up on me, yet here is Taylor's little friend Kali. She doesn't weigh much, so I'll pretend that's how she got the jump on me. She's clearly light on her feet.

Keeping my eyes on the water, I blow out a line of smoke and then tell her, "Invisible? She's only visible when she deems it's worth her time. You're not worth her time."

Kali surprises me by sitting in the mud next to me. "What's got you more sour than usual?"

"None of your fucking business."

"Lee, I take it? Taylor called me. Don't worry, she didn't say much, never does. Whatever brainwashing tactics y'all use are impressive."

I ignore the brainwashing comment. "If she didn't tell you anything, how do you know it's Lee?"

"Because I'm not an idiot. You hate the guy. He's been sweet on Taylor, more often as of late."

I shrug and smile. Allison is still watching us, hidden all but her glowing, yellow eyes. "I'd love nothing more than to slit Lee's throat."

"God, you're such a baby. All of you Delta what the fuck ever Theta boys are so spoiled that you can't share anyone's affections. Lee can't be friends with Taylor and your brother because you're so insecure that you need *all* of their attention. Pathetic."

This fucking bitch. I wasn't bothering a damn soul out here. I left the house to avoid violence. "Kali?"

"Yes?"

"Go fuck yourself. In the ass. With no lube."

"How about you try it? You might actually like it." She smirks at me. Her red hair lightly flowing in the breeze.

"You're braver, or stupider, than most people."

"Nah. I just know that you won't do shit."

"My reputation says otherwise." Hell, Allison is *right there*. I could feed her this bitch, and we'd both be happy.

Kali leans in and whispers. "Taylor. I'm her *only* friend. Would you really kill her best friend after she just lost Lois?"

Despite my shitty day I chuckle and take a hit off my smoke. "You got me there. You fucking got me."

"I know. I've got you by the balls, Soren." She reaches over and pulls the cigarette from between my fingers.

"For now," I warn her. One day Taylor might drop this bitch, and I'll be there.

"And as Taylor's best friend, *for now*," she mimics my voice, "I think you need to get over whatever is going on. You almost lost your brother, dickhead. You almost lost Taylor. Everyone is literally fucking dying, and instead of living with what time is left, you're out here sitting in the mud and sulking. Grow up."

She doesn't know that my brother wants to fuck my girlfriend with his best friend. I wonder if she'd have the same response. Either way, that bold bitch has a point. *That's annoying*.

"Besides," she continues, "just let everyone know you're the alpha male, and claim your dominance. Think of it as your pack."

"My pack?"

"Yeah. Like a wolf pack."

I burst out laughing. "Thanks for the pep talk." Before she has a chance to spew any more unwanted advice, I stand up. Admittedly though, Taylor's little friend did make some valid points, and she's right. Time is fleeting. I won't waste any more of it. I'm going to make the most of it with the people who matter.

We're a family, a pack. And, I *am* the fucking alpha.

I swallow trying to wet my dry throat. I don't need to be nervous. I'm the alpha here. I can do this. It's not like I'm a spoiled brat who can't share. *I really don't want to fucking share.* Wait. No. I'm an alpha, not a brat. If anyone is the brat, it's fucking Lee. However, if my brother and mouse want him as their play toy, then so be it. Alpha's take care of their own. Those two are the only family I genuinely care about.

If they say yes, Lee gets to breathe another day. If they say no... Allison and I have a dinner date.

When I enter the bedroom, the three of them are all fully dressed and sitting on Steffan's bed whispering. Of course they immediately stop. "Like it's not fucking obvious you three were just talking shit about me." My eyes are trained on Steffan's midnight blue ones. "What do you want?" Steffan's blond brows furrow so I ask again. "What do you *want*?"

"What do you mean?" he asks, but he knows. My twin knows exactly what I'm asking him. But if he wants me to pull it out of him, I can do that, too. "Fine." I take a few more steps into the room. "*Who* do you want?"

Steffan's throat bobs as he swallows. "I... want whatever everyone else wants."

Of course you do. Self- sacrificing Saint Carmichael. But even saints have needs. I know. He knows. We all know, but I want him to say it, and we all know where we fucking stand. Because if he doesn't have the balls to claim Lee as his fuck buddy, then I sure as hell am not sharing Taylor with him. Either he's worth me putting up with, or he's not. "Bullshit. My patience is already being tested. Don't fucking push it, brother. Do you want to fuck everyone in this room, or not? Are you going along with this for him? Are you doing this so he can have Taylor? Or so you can have Taylor *and* him?"

"Yes." Steffan didn't specify which, but I know Steffan well enough.

I turn my eyes to Lee and command, "Get undressed." I look back to my brother. "We do this, there will be rules. But I'm too pissed right now." My gaze softens as it lands on Taylor. "Little mouse, do you want to play with Lee?"

"Yes," she tells me.

"Then be a good girl, and undress for me. I need to bury myself deep. Will you let me?"

"Yes."

"Good."

I begin to undress, and so does Steffan. Standing there with a full erection, I look at Lee and Steffan and scoff, "A psychopath, a martyr, and a prince. Let's find out who fucks the best."

Taylor comes over and loops her arms around my neck. "I'm glad you came back."

Her fingertips trail down my chest until they wrap around my cock. She's going to make me lose my fucking mind. Steffan comes to stand behind her. He peppers kisses down her spine causing her to tighten her hold around my neck. Steffan kneels down behind her. Taylor hangs on to me as he spreads her legs. The wet sound of his tongue inside her has my balls tightening. She lets out a gasp as her body shivers.

"That's enough." I have to force the words out. Not that I mind what was happening, but I need to maintain control. At least for this first time. "Get back on the bed, Steffan."

I go and sit on the chair where Taylor had been the first time I came into the room. I pat my lap. "Come sit with me, little mouse. Brother Concord." Lee raises his eyebrows in acknowledgment. "Go suck your president's cock."

Lee and Steffan stare at each other, and the tension is crackling. Their hard cocks twitch as their chests rapidly rise and fall. Fuck me sideways, this shit is hot. Both of them are evidently nervous as hell despite the sexual chemistry that's filling the room. The *will they, won't they* suspense of it all has me on the edge of my seat.

I slide my hand up Taylor's thigh and relish her audible intake of breath. My hand teases her as I creep up higher but not to the sweet spot. Both of us keep our eyes trained on Lee as he finally brings his head down toward Steffan's painfully raging hard cock. Steffan hisses as Lee blows on his glistening head. As Lee's mouth takes Steffan to the hilt, I insert two fingers into Taylor. Her breath stutters as I circle the little nub with my thumb, and I keep my fingers in sync with Lee. She's still soaking from Steffan's tongue. Her back arches and I kiss her neck. My own cock is beginning to soak my leg as Taylor's pussy clamps around my fingers, and Steffan moans and grabs a fistful of Lee's thick locks. Lee's eyes are closed, and he licks at Steffan's dick like it's the most delicious nectar and it's giving him life.

"Lee. Fuck. Yes," Steffan pants.

"Shh. I've got you," Lee tells him.

"I know you do. Fuck, do I know."

My throat is getting tight with how much I'm enjoying this. I help Taylor stand and then take her by the hand to the bed. I position her behind Lee. "While Lee is choking on Steffan's cock, I want you to play with Lee's balls and asshole."

"What are you going to do?" she purrs.

Oh sweet little mouse. I'm going to do what I do best. "I'm going to fuck you from behind. *Hard*."

Lee moans as Taylor's tongue licks the back of his nuts. "Spit on your fingers and stick them in. Please, baby," Steffan moans.

I can hear the smile in Lee's voice as he asks Steffan. "You like that? You want me to finger your ass, too?"

"Yes," Steffan grunts.

Taylor is already wet so I don't waste any time. That is my new motto on life – *Don't waste time. Be the fucking alpha.* I drive into her in one thrust. I grip her shoulder with one hand and hold her hips in place as I give her my full force. I make good on my word that I was going to be fucking her hard. This causes her to push harder into Lee. Steffan and I make eye contact, and I give him a smirk. *You're welcome, fucker.* Thanks to me, he's getting everyone. Sure, Lee was about to get the balls to make a move, but would they have actually done anything if I hadn't pushed it? I'd like to think not. This is my doing. I might've protested at first, but at the end of the day, I gave my brother this. Steffan's happiness always comes first. Taylor's happiness always comes first. Lee's happiness...I don't give two shits about.

Taylor cries out, her pussy already too sensitive from coming earlier, and I continue to pump harder into her. One hand leaves Lee to reach behind and grab my thigh. I grip her wrist and say, "We've got you."

I trail my fingertips down her spine like she did my chest earlier. *Beautiful.* I look down at my body connecting to hers, in and out. Gliding easily through that wet pussy. I spit on my finger and then play with her ass. That sends her body quivering. Her pussy has me in a tight grip as her head falls forward and her breathing becomes ragged. She's falling apart on my dick, and sends a surge of satisfaction through me. Between that and Steffan's moan of release, I begin coming hard into Taylor's sweet pussy.

Lee groans in pleasure, ruining the mood. “Shut the fuck up,” I grumble.

Thankfully, Taylor moans again. I close my eyes with a sigh and bite my bottom lip as she continues to come around my dick. *Because I’m the fucking alpha.*

CHAPTER FOURTEEN

Lee

Life is fucking weird sometimes. One minute everything is figured out, and the next it's all sideways. All it took was one look from her deep brown eyes, and a swipe of her tongue over her bottom lip, for everything to change. There is no going back on what happened between all of us. I don't regret a single second, but I'm not sure where we go from here. My eyes touch on the man who is my best friend, even while I remember how his cock tasted in my mouth while Taylor's soft hands pumped pleasure from mine. I glance over at his ice-cold twin and remember the way he orchestrated the whole scene and brought us all to admit the things we wanted. A part of me is smart enough to not fully trust Soren. He's a wild animal. For now it seems he's fine with me, but he could turn on me any minute. The only people he's loyal to are Steffan and Taylor.

I should be concerned about the current job we're on, but my mind is just completely screwed. Thinking about last night filters into my mind while I fight to remain composed. This is the first job we've done without The Illicit's knowledge. After what happened in my family home, it was decided we needed more ammunition for just us. The games of our fathers have become messy.

"Are we one hundred percent sure of this plan?" Soren asks, his tone bored, even while his eyes stay focused on the elevator shaft that our associates will be arriving in. From our position in the offices above, we can intercept them if they try to take advantage.

"Walter encouraged it," I respond,and roll my shoulders back. Much to his dismay, I actually do my homework on our runs and projects before sending our guys in. I am nothing but thorough, which is how I've survived my family and risen to the rank I have within the Brotherhood.

"So you said," Soren scoffs and twists his neck. "And this was after your dad shot your mom?"

My mom's face flashes in my mind once again. The glazed look in her eyes, and the silent way she tried to communicate with me before taking her last breath. "Yes, after. She spilled his dirty secret, and he shot her before she could tell me all of it. Thanks for bringing it up, dick."

Soren scoffs and uses his gun to scratch the back of his head, "Your dad must be fucking desperate about something."

"Sore." Steffan's voice reaches his brother, reminding him that some information is sacred, and also to settle the room. Besides my own festering anger, I can tell Jose is on edge.

I peer at him out of the side of my eye. "I take it my sister filled you in, Succo."

Jose's outer demeanor looks stoic, but after training the man for half a year, I can tell that his body is tightly coiled under his black sweater. His eyes touch on all of us. "She refuses to plan the funeral, or make arrangements, until The Illicit decides the punishment for your father. She doesn't want him there or to pretend that he is sympathetic."

"Sounds like a shit position to be in, Jose." Soren chuckles and lights up his cigarette.

Jose barely acknowledges him, only shifting his weight to his other leg before leaning back against the wall. Jose remains as loyal to my sister as he is to the Brotherhood. Something he also hides from the families. I'm ready for his initiation to be over so that they can stop hiding, and my sister can openly have his support, the support and care that she needs. Right now his care for her has been closely concealed as helping her recover from her attack.

I've been a piece of shit brother to her. I need to call and check in on her. She's so independent and strong, that sometimes I forget how much she hides her emotions. Chanda is so much like our mother. Graceful. Beautiful. Strong. To think she almost suffered the same fate as our mother. Being married to a monster until he's ready to dispose of her. That too, was our father's doing. Luckily, he was murdered, and now she has Jose.

"We'll figure out a plan," Steffan chimes in. His eyes collide with mine. "Your dad isn't going to get away with it. And then we will find out about the missing child."

"Unless that child has already found us," Soren speaks up again, his hand rubbing along his jaw.

Jose's gaze sharpens on Soren. "You think the child is connected to taking out members?"

"That would be a stretch." Soren laughs at his own thought. "I just meant maybe the child was looking and happened to find your family, Lee. Or else how would your mother have known? Maybe that was what else she wanted to reveal, but wasn't able to do."

That day moves to the front of my memories again, the same rushing feeling of emotions causes a riot in my chest. My father definitely feared the truth, and my mom was angry enough to have told it. But he didn't seem shocked that she knew. What made her decide to tell now?

"I need to do some searching of my own. If there really is a Concord child out there, then there has to be a reason that they were hidden."

"True," Soren jumps in. "It's not like our families hide their bastard children, only that they don't make it into The Illicit."

Steffan's gaze jumps between the both of us, and I can see him taking everything in and pondering it. "I still think we're missing something."

Jose glances between all of us, and I can tell his next few words weigh on him heavily. "What if we're grouping things together that aren't related?"

"Explain," Steffan says, his gaze focused on the doors.

"We've grouped the late murders with the things that are happening to the Concord family, but what if they're different?" Jose shrugs his shoulders. "One seems to be for power while the other is more personal. We've always wondered if this is a two-person job."

"Well, Bryce Van Doren has been eliminated," I add, "and so was Alex Dupree."

"What if the fifth family has never been as far away as we think they are?" Jose speaks and the silence in the room is deafening. We all mull over what he said, and what it could mean. The fifth founding family. They've not been mentioned in years, and even before that they were talked about as if they were a myth. What could that family have to do with my father? Are they somehow connected to Taylor? The Van Dorens? Duprees? None of this is making any sense. The dots are all over the place with no rhyme or reason to connect them.

"Our father always said there was no coming back for the family. The whole bloodline was wiped out," Steffan answers, and I notice the way his gaze gets a faraway look, as if he's really contemplating it. He knows as well as I do, our fathers have also lied – especially if it was in their best interest.

"Yes." I glance between them all. "But, why? Your father said it was bad blood, mine says it was that the power wasn't distributed equally. Record books from that time indicate that the Boudreaux family made a grave mistake, and overstepped the laws of The Illicit and were consequently wiped out."

Even saying their name gives me the creeps. The Boudreaux family is only a name whispered among The Illicit. Everyone is borderline superstitious that bad luck will bestow the family for even speaking the name.

"Bad blood," Soren mutters under his breath. "Or blood for blood?"

Blood for blood. That was the last message received. My heart hammers in my ribcage, and the possibility of ending this war with a faceless person becomes more attainable. "After this, we need to focus more of our energy on looking into the fifth family. Whether or not I have another sibling running around can wait. If we're going to step into our roles in The Illicit, we need the rule of our fathers cleansed first. We need to find the killer and end this once and for all."

The door to the elevator shaft vibrates as the elevator starts ascending. Jose starts looking at his cameras and outside security before glancing back at us. "The field is clean. The brothers are doing a sweep. This looks promising."

Steffan moves forward, and we watch as members of the Bloodhound gang step onto the dusty ground, hands on their weapons, and look around. When they seem to be satisfied about not finding an ambush, their leader, Mac Diablo, steps out. Steffan walks to the stairs and starts going down. Soren follows, and then I'm last. Jose stays to remain in contact with our security and other brothers.

"Nice that you could join us, Diablo," Steffan greets him.

Diablo and his men step forward, and even though their position is guarded, Mac Diablo's face is anything but. I can see his smirk and a glint of approval in his eye as he steps closer to us.

"Finally out of your father's shadow, huh?" He scratches his fingers along the black goatee on his chin. "I was surprised to see the location change, and that my name was changed on the order shipment. For as long as I have been working with the Carmichaels and The Illicit, my name has always been Rojo Tiger."

Steffan's shoulders relax a fraction, and the smirk on his lips is the most casual he dares to wear around any of our associates. Soren tenses, but doesn't take his eyes off Diablo. "My father's pyramid of names is not only degrading, but also meant to abuse that power."

Diablo arches a brow. "And with him being dead now, I take it you're on a different path?"

I share a glance with Soren who takes a step forward toward his brother. I step next, showing solidarity, but also as a reminder that Steffan doesn't act alone. "We're not out to cause trouble. We just think this job, and your products, are better handled by us, rather than the lackey crew that would have been sent now that Rhett Carmichael is gone."

Diablo's eyes rest on me for just a second before scanning over all of us again. This is the first, and only time, anyone has stepped out of the normalcy for The Illicit and mentioned the way our fathers have treated their associates who are not of The Illicit. "The way I see it, now is the perfect time to move on from The Illicit entirely. Maybe the war within will finally take your Brotherhood to its expiration point."

Soren grunts, "A war within only means that a stronger generation will rise. Do you really want to be on the bad side of that legacy?"

Diablo's eyes run over the prickly Carmichael twin before glancing again at his brother and finally me. I let myself relax, and my expression grow bored, as if this conversation holds no weight on my chest. We need this shipment from Diablo to turn the tides to us, and for others to start seeing us separately. If they decide to turn on us, it will get back to the current elders. It's a fine line between life and death.

"You young ones have balls. I'll give you that. But – you still have a lot to learn. Don't get overconfident." He stares us down. Nobody flinches, or allows our body language to give us away. Just when I think he's going to tell us to fuck off, he speaks. "I want an extra three percent next time. I am carrying your message after all," Diablo bargains, which is something we expected. While three percent might not sound like a lot, it's enough to keep him highly paid in his part of the world, in addition to what he sells.

"We can make that work." Steffan nods his head. "Provided that the message is delivered clearly."

Diablo nods his head and motions his first-in-command over to take the envelope that Steffan offers. Diablo steps up next, and the two men shake hands. "I look forward to our next meeting."

I watch as the Bloodhounds and Diablo get back in the elevator and descend to the basement. After a few minutes, Jose jumps down to our floor. "It's all clear."

"Keep a close watch on him until the next shipment date. If we're going to do this, we need to be smart. Others will follow as long as there is good standing between us and the Bloodhounds," Steffan says, and I nod along.

It's done. Our first official business outside of the current reign of The Illicit. This is a gesture that can't be taken back. It's our turn for power, whether the current elders like it, or not.

"Succo, you can leave first," Soren suddenly says, and we all stop from leaving. Steffan and I turn to face Soren.

Jose's brow lifts, and he glances my way. I give him a small nod, and without glancing back he keeps moving. It's not until the elevator door shuts behind him does Soren continue. The twin's eyes have gone colder, if possible. His face is blank, and if I didn't know Soren like I do, I would be ready to fight. The man in front of us has completely changed. The only word my mind can think of is *murderer*.

"What is it?" Steffan asks, a frown on his face while he looks over his brother.

"We need to settle this matter before we keep moving on. You were both there last night, it's not like I have to remind you," Soren speaks, each and every word is laced with a deadly edge to it.

"What about it?" Steffan sighs and runs his hands through his hair. I wonder if this is as soul changing for him as it is for me.

"I want rules, and I want an answer. We started this deal with Taylor first, and we agreed how to spend time with her. If she wants Lee, I'll let her make time for him, but both of you need to know now that I'm not willing to share much else."

"If she wants any part of me, I'll give her my all," the words are out of my mouth before I can think about it further. The fact that I have wanted Taylor for months is not lost on me. She was the only one who was able to heal me, and through her kindness, I formed an obsession for her like no other. "I won't push past your guys' boundaries, or relationship with her, but if she wants me, too, she can have me."

"So you want her," Soren asks and steps closer.

"Yes," I breathe out the word that lives in my heart when it comes to Taylor.

Soren's eyes move over every part of my face, my body, before glancing at his brother. "I will only be okay with this, all of this, on one condition. You can't give her your tie."

I feel the weight of his command on my chest, but it makes no difference. The significance isn't lost on me, I already chose someone once for my tie, and she died brutally at the hands of her brother. Soren needs this, and to keep the peace with him and his brother, I have to be willing to accept his condition. Even without my tie, it doesn't sever the connection I already have with her.

"I can accept this." I hold Soren's gaze and can feel when the tension leaves the room.

"I will do anything for Taylor, and that means if she wants all three of us, she gets all three of us." Steffan glances between his brother and myself. "So no one better be a jackass about it. And anything that happens in any of our rooms does not make it past those doors. We protect her above all else."

I nod in agreement, and even Soren agrees with his brother. Without a final look back, Steffan steps into the elevator. Soren follows, and so do I. We came in here with one goal, and we're leaving with a whole new outlook. Again, all I can think is…life really is fucking *weird* sometimes.

CHAPTER FIFTEEN

Taylor

It's been two days since I saw the guys last. If not for the text from Steffan letting me know they had some private business to attend to, I would have felt used. That night was a new brand on my soul, and all over my skin. Skin they had touched, kissed, claimed, and then left. There were no explanations or discussions. Besides Soren verbally detailing what was happening to my body, and things I witnessed, no one talked about it afterward. I had no idea what we were now. A foursome? Was that a thing? Would they both still want me after sharing me with their only friend? Little voices begin to whisper words of doubt and insecurity in my mind. I was raised that a lady keeps her knees together and only gives her heart to one man... forever. My knees were spread miles apart and my heart passed around like a sample platter. It was so hot, though. The pleasure was unbelievable. The chemistry, undeniable. Yet, now that time has passed I'm wondering if they'll think less of me somehow. The more I think about it, the more I question myself. What happened to the small town good girl? I went from virgin, to three men at once, in less than a year. What about Lee? If the intent wasn't to include him into our relationship, was I just used as a place for him to not feel lonely? I don't know what to believe, or how to feel, and the only two assholes who can clue me in on anything, are gone. Saving the campus or something.

With a sigh, I head to my last class of the day and force myself to feel normal. Even as I try, I can feel the lingering gazes, the whispers follow me around the halls. It's not as though Steffan and Soren have been quiet about our relationship, and I have never felt the need to hide it either. Until they aren't here, and I lose some of my usual bravado and confidence. Without meaning to, I pass the front doors of the library, and halt in my tracks. Lois's eyes and colorful smile are forever ingrained in my mind. Her death didn't leave me the time to properly grieve her. She was taken too soon, and there are still so many wicked things I wanted to learn from her. That woman lit up the world in the most spectacular of ways.

I grab my phone out of my pocket and pull up Kali's name. A girls' night is needed, and since the guys have left my mind spinning, I need the ultimate distraction.

ME: Movie and popcorn tonight?

It doesn't take long for the dots to start bouncing, and her instant reply brings a smile to my lips.

Kali: Hell to the yeah, bitch! I need some girl time. I have just the movie for us ;-)

With a smile on my face, I finally move past the library and find my class. I just have to sit through a two-hour lecture on forbidden media, and then I can sink back into my thoughts and let my guard down. If anyone can help me process my mind fuck, it will be Kali. My best friend is always good at spinning my worst nightmare around so that I can breathe again.

Kali and I are lounging in the home theater at the mansion. None of the brothers ever use the home theater that's in the basement. It's amazing and always stocked with snacks and drinks, so Kali and I love making use of it. She wanted to go back to our place, but I'm still skittish after being attacked on the track and football field.

Kali has caught me up on all the latest gossip around campus, and about everyone in all our classes while we gathered our snacks and popped popcorn. Finally she releases an overly dramatic sigh. "So you don't want to talk about it?" Kali's brow shoots up, and her head tilts confused. About as confused as I am myself.

"No," I huff and fall onto the giant cozy couch sized reclining theater seat. "But, yes. I do, but I'm not ready."

"I see," she hums and sits down with the bowl of popcorn in her lap. I fling my arm over my eyes and inhale the buttery goodness smell. My other hand reaches out and grabs a few pieces and pops them into my mouth.

"No, no I don't. I want to eat popcorn and watch a movie with my best friend tonight. I don't know why

I spend so much time worried about these men when they just take off at the drop of a hat without considering my feelings."

Kali giggles next to me. "And there is the first issue I'm guessing. Those two idiots still haven't figured out that the communication needs to happen after the group sex? A girl still needs to be cuddled."

"Kali!" I laugh and laugh until my cheeks hurt from smiling. I also start to feel better. "They really are idiots. All three of them." Immediately I regret the words as soon as they leave my mouth.

Kali goes still next to me, the popcorn in her hand freezing on her way to her mouth. Her eyes widen. "Three?"

No. No. No. This is bad. I feel terrible. In my own pity party, I almost forgot that Kali always had a flirty and easygoing manner with Lee. She's never said it out loud, but I often wondered if she likes him. She's denied it, but I swear I see a look of disappointment in her eyes. "It was just a one-time thing. I'm not even sure if it meant anything, or if I was just helping him not feel lonely."

She sits up straighter, and her eyes fall to the popcorn bowl. "It's not like you owe me any explanations or anything, Tay. We're not a couple, nor have we really talked much outside of being at the house because a killer is after us." She laughs it off, but my gut sinks further.

"I know you two talk." They were even texting for a while. I haven't asked if they still do. Honestly, I haven't been great at communication either. I'm the worst friend. "I guess I never really asked. Do you like Lee?"

A small smile pulls at her lips, "I think if this was a different world, that didn't involve murder, The Illicit Brotherhood, or my amazing best friend, I could like him. Right now he's just always hit me as the peacemaker. He's always so put together. I like to ruffle his feathers when he's around."

Ruffling feathers is her specialty it seems. Kali is one of those people who glows and makes life fun. That's simply who she is. The thought that I've just ruined our friendship is devastating. Who have I become? I've become so consumed with The Illicit and these guys, that I've ignored everyone else's feelings. Not everyone. My best and only friend.

"Kali, your friendship means everything to me. If this is an issue, I will step away so I don't hurt you. Hoes before bros, right?" I sit up, and my hand touches her arm gently. I can't mess this up. I refuse to lose the person who has been my savior since the day I met her.

"I think you are way too outnumbered by dick to say that anymore." Kali laughs, and I can't help but join her. "But seriously, Taylor, this isn't something to ruin friendships over. Maybe I could have liked Lee, in a different world, yes. In this world, he isn't what I need. He's what you need, and in all honesty, he needs you more."

She grabs more popcorn and keeps eating while her eyes stay on me. I toss the idea around in my head, and wonder if she's right about him needing me more. Maybe I'm selfish, but I like the idea. I don't want to give up whatever this is that is growing between them and me. I want to hold onto the happiness I feel when

I'm with them, and the way I feel desired every time they look at me.

But I need to be here with my friend right now. I refuse to allow my attention to stray anywhere else. "Alright," I finally say, conceding to her. "Well, now that that is out of the way, let's get on with our girls' night. It's been way too long."

"It really has." Kali laughs and grabs the remote to start the movie. "You know in between all the death, the funerals, destruction, and hospital visits, there really hasn't been time."

My head tilts back, and I join her in something between a groan and laugh, as morbid as it sounds, "I wonder what a normal college experience is like?"

"I think more college girls would be interested in shuffling around three boyfriends like you are."

"Ugh." My curls fall over my forehead. "Is that what I'm doing even? I thought it was insane to have two. I just figured that their twin instincts were working together to make it work for all of us." Despite myself, I can't stop talking about them. I'd told myself I was going to make tonight all about me and Kali. Yet, here I go again, talking about them. Still, it feels good to have someone to confide in. "The boys have alpha personalities, but they wear it differently. I don't know what's happening with Lee, to be honest. For all I know, it could be a one-time thing."

Kali pushes pause on the remote and turns to me, her eyes squinting in concentration. "I think they're guys who have a lot going on, and that they didn't leave to hurt your feelings. When they get back, they'll find a way to talk about it. And this gives you the time to decide what you want to do. I don't think they would have made the decision without thinking about how it would affect you. They're crazy about you."

She's right. Even though my stomach is in knots, and I have so many thoughts still bouncing around, I can't do anything until we can talk. "Okay, let's start the movie. What are we watching?"

"Well, keeping up with the times, I got us a 90's slasher movie." Kali grins and hits play.

Great. Because it's not like I'm living in a real-life slasher movie.

CHAPTER SIXTEEN

Lee

I follow behind Steffan and Soren as we enter the house and find Jose already up and operating with his computer system everywhere. Maximus, one of our other strong technical guys, is bent over with him while they look at lists.

"What are you doing, Scab?" Soren drawls while scowling at the screen. Steffan walks over and looks at the screens, as well.

"I'm pulling more information for us. I'm looking for all children born between our births and the time the fifth family was wiped out. And I'm cross referencing all those names to known associates, people in The Illicit, and others who have gone to Thorn University," Jose explains.

Steffan's brow rises, and Soren manages to look legitimately proud. "Color me impressed, Scab."

I scoff and slap a hand on Jose's shoulder. "Let us know when it's ready."

He nods in agreement, and I walk away, needing a shower, and then needing to see our girl. Leaving right after everything we experienced didn't feel right. I don't want Taylor hung up on us leaving, because we always will be. She needs to know I'll always come back to her, and so will Soren and Steffan.

After quickly washing up, I grab a T-shirt and flannel before slipping on a pair of jeans. I grab my phone and see that Taylor did text back to the group to let us know she's at her house. Frustrated that she's out of reach, and also dying to see her, I quickly open my text to the messages between Soren, Steffan, and myself.

ME: I'm seeing her first.

SOREN: This is the only time.

STEFFAN: Bring her over when you're done.

With that go-ahead, I grab my keys and wallet before jogging down the stairs and out the door. She'd been staying here, but I guess after her movie night with her friend, she decided to go back to her house. Taylor's place isn't far from the house, but with the current climate of danger, none of us like when she is this far away. She does have a good roommate with her at least. There's something about Kali. She's fierce. We've had our fair share of conversations, and I enjoy her company. It always feels like she wants more, though. Unfortunately I can't give her that. No doubt we have a connection. Maybe if I hadn't had the year from hell, who knows what might've been. Taylor and Steffan are the only two who can bring me peace.

Within a few minutes, I arrive and pull up to the house. Kali's car is gone, and it makes me feel a little better knowing I'm going to get Taylor all to myself. She answers the door before I even get a chance to knock. While her smile is hesitant, everything on my face gives away how I feel. My eyes sweep over her body, taking in the leggings and long Thorn University T-shirt, before coming back to her face. Taylor's cheeks are rosy, but I can read the uncertainty in her eyes. My heart thuds painfully in my chest, wanting her to open up to me, while at the same time realizing that we're treading on new ground.

"Hi," I manage to get out, and her lips twitch a little. Of all the things that need to be said, I lead with hi. "Can we talk?"

"Yeah," She answers, her eyes falling to the floor as she moves out of the way to let me in. I follow her into the house and up the stairs to her room. Of all the times I've been here, there has never been the tension I feel right now. Her body practically screams at me to say something, and I will. Once we get behind a closed door and can have some privacy, just in case Kali is home. Everything I have to say I want her to hear first, to be the only one to hear it from me.

Taylor shuts the door to her room behind us, and her hands clasp together in front of her body. "Did everything work out okay with your business things?"

My brow raises, and I almost forget for a second about how much Soren and Steffan actually tell her. Taylor isn't a doll in the life of an Illicit brother, she is the making of a queen. "It was better than we expected.

I don't speak for the other two, but I am sorry we had to leave so soon. I had wanted to talk with you, but when Steffan got the call, we had to make a move."

"I get it." Her voice is full of understanding. I hope she sincerely does get it. It's easy in the beginning, to think you're on board with this life, but after stuff happens time and again. Some couples don't last because of the uncertainty. The Brotherhood either brings you together, or drives a wedge between relationships.

She sits on the edge of her bed and looks me directly in the eye when she speaks. "I do want to have that talk, though."

I move to kneel in front of her. My hand reaches out, and I slide my hand into hers. "Taylor, that night meant more to me than you'll ever know. I've felt a connection with you since the first time we hung out. I was a mess, but with you, I didn't have to hide it. I got to experience my emotions, deal with the grief, and find my true meaning. I was ready to move on. The other night wasn't me being lonely in the way you think it was. It wasn't pining for what my best friend has that I don't."

"What was it then?" she asks, her bottom lip caught between her teeth, and tears shine in her eyes.

"I wanted you, too, and I never thought I could have a chance," I admit, and the truth feels so good. "I was jealous that my best friend and his brother had you to themselves, when all I could think about every day was the taste of your lips, or the smell of your hair in the sunshine. I was lonely, but I was lonely over you."

"How will this work?" She asks, getting to her feet and pacing to the other side of her room.

I stand on my own and leave my hands at my sides. "We talked about it, and if you are willing to accept me, then Steffan is okay with it, and Soren will live with it."

A nervous laugh escapes from her. *Soren will live with it.* We both know he doesn't tolerate anything that displeases him for very long.

"He's willing to live with it, I should say. For now."

Our eyes lock across the space, and she confesses. "I don't think I could bear to be without any of you, now that I know what it feels like. I was scared I ruined everything, that I was too greedy."

"There was nothing for you to ruin. We are the ones who can't let you go," I step toward her and take her hand in mine, before placing it on my chest right over where my heart beats for her. "You can be as selfish as you want with me."

Her eyes widen, but then surprise quickly replaces itself with lust and want. I can't wait anymore, the need to have her again, taste her again, as mine is too big a temptation to be ignored. My hands slide to her face, and with one last look into her deep, chocolatey eyes, my lips crash down on hers. She moans in surprise, her hands finding their way to my shoulders where she clutches me. I slide one arm around her waist, pulling her body into mine. Her mouth opens, inviting me in. My tongue touches hers, sliding together, devouring each other.

I walk her back to the bed, and when her knees hit the edge I let her go. Her body lands, and her lips pop open in surprise. I only give her a second of uncertainty before I start taking off my flannel and the T-shirt underneath. I watch through hooded eyes as Taylor's gaze takes in every inch of exposed skin I show her.

"Undress for me, baby." Our eyes catch, and I see the way the color in her cheeks deepens. Her hands move her leggings down her body while I step out of my jeans at the same time. I can't take my eyes off her when she lifts the material of her T-shirt off, and it lands in a pool with the rest of our clothes by her bedside.

Unlike last time, I get to take my time appreciating her body, and all the ways I want to worship her with my fingers, my tongue, and my cock. Slowly, my hands run over her calves and up her legs, enjoying the way her breathing turns shallow and her lips part while she watches me move higher. I stop my hands on her thighs and force her legs to open wider. "I'm going to taste you first, baby girl. It's my one regret about last time."

Without giving her the chance to answer, I drop to my arms and devour her, desperate to fill my stomach with her taste. Taylor's legs shake, and her back arches. The sweetest moans fall from her lips while she bucks into my face. Lust tightens in my stomach, and my hands grip her hips tighter.

"Lee," she purrs my name while I shove two fingers inside her, stroking and curling to find that special spot inside to drive her wild. It's the sweetest sound I've ever heard. I want Taylor at my mercy while she comes undone. With every stroke of my tongue and my lips on her clit, she climbs higher and higher. I love keeping her dancing on my fingers, pushing her toward her climax slowly, completely under my control.

"I think I love you best this way, Tay. Soft, pliant, your pussy strangling my fingers while your taste coats my tongue. Are you thinking about the last time? Or are you thinking about just me?"

"You," she gasps, but the way she grows wetter with every word I say, I think she likes thinking about the other night, too.

"I bet they'd be so jealous right now. If they could see what I get to see. The adorable flush on your chest, the way your legs are shaking, the way your eyes can't stay focused because you feel so out of your mind with pleasure."

She moans, and her hips buck fast against my face. Not that I'm lying about anything I'm saying. Taylor close to an impending orgasm is a sight to see. My fingers pump faster into her pretty pussy, curling and rubbing against her insides. "If they were here, I wouldn't let them join this time, Taylor. I'd make them watch. Soren would be pissy and would probably sit in your desk chair. He'd watch and take his cock out, stroking it, but you'd like that. And Steffan," I moan a little thinking of my best friend. "He'd try and participate. But eventually he'd see how well I'm keeping their little mouse pleased. He'd lean against the wall and pump his cock watching us. They would only get to watch. This time is for me and for you. I want you to know exactly how much you mean to me. How I have as much of a claim over you as they do. You want me, too, don't you, baby?"

"Yes!" she screams, and her back bows off the bed, my words, and the vision of her two other boyfriends watching us, finally sending her spinning into pleasure.

I drag my fingers out of her before sucking the juices off my fingers.

"I'll never get tired of how good you taste, baby."

"Lee," she whimpers my name, and her arms reach for me. I finish undressing, taking my time, my eyes never leaving hers. I join her, my body looming over hers. I place a kiss on her jaw, her cheek, and finally on her soft lips. Taylor kisses me back frantically, lovingly, until her breaths are mine, and mine are hers. My cock aches to be inside of her, precum leaks onto her skin between us. I don't stop kissing her until my hands have touched every part of her bare body, and she's frantically moving under me, looking for more friction on her needy little clit.

"You're mine, Taylor." I wrap my hand around her throat.

Her brown eyes widen, and her lips, now puffy and red, part. I pull her up to her knees and help her to straddle my lap so she's above me. Her hands land on my shoulders, and her fingers tighten on the skin there, the nails biting. I like the pain and the way she clutches me, even while I'm cutting off her air supply, she's trusting and pliant. Using my free hand, I guide my cock to her opening and run the head against her glistening pussy lips.

"Please," Taylor whispers, her hips trying frantically to pull me in.

"Say it first," I tell her, holding her body above mine, waiting, driving us both insane when all I want is to thrust into her and make us one.

Her eyes shine while they dart around my face, and she's so easy to read. She wants this. She's as greedy for me as I am for her, and now that we have Soren and Steffan's blessing, she's going to be insatiable. "I want you. Please fuck me."

Her words create shivers down my spine. My head falls back as I moan. "Mmm, I'll fucking make love to you, baby." I let go of her hip at the same time I shove my cock inside of her. The smacking sound of our flesh resonates in the room, and the little cry from her mouth sets me off.

My hand flexes around her throat with every flex of my hips. I let her ride me, her hips grinding and pulling, like she wants to take the life out of me through my dick. I bet we'd be a sight to see right now. Imagining Soren and Steffan witnessing me with our girl does something to me. I thrust faster, deeper, until Taylor is crying my name, and her hands are gripping my shoulders, my neck, wildly.

I watch where my cock disappears into her, the way her stomach tightens and flexes with every bounce she makes in my lap, the way her tits sway and move, the little nipples thrust toward my lips, begging for attention, and finally to the red marks on her skin where my hand grips her, leaving evidence of what I did. I might not be able to give her my blue tie, but I can give her a different kind of jewelry to wear.

Taylor's next orgasm rolls through her on a silent cry, her insides clamping around my cock and pulling my own release from me.

"Jesus...fuck," I pant, my spine tingling, while she moans in satisfaction. I come hard inside her, letting go of her neck so both my hands can hold her hips and keep our bodies pressed together. "You're amazing, baby. You're so beautiful," I tell her while placing kisses over her chest and shoulders.

We collapse onto her bed, and Taylor throws her blanket around us. "I have no words right now. That was so good."

I chuckle and cuddle her close. "I need to lay here for a minute."

"You could stay the night," she whispers, leaning up on her hand, bringing her gaze to mine.

I push her hair back from her face, a softening in my chest that I never felt before grips my heart. "Yeah. That sounds perfect."

I pull her close and right as her arm bands around my waist, her bedroom door opens. "Oh, shit! Ahhh, so sorry guys." Kali backs out and closes the door behind her.

I fight the urge to laugh until I see the look of horror on Taylor's face. "Oh, fuck, what's wrong, baby?" She looks like she could cry, and the last thing I ever want is her to be sad.

"Nothing. I'm just being stupid," She bites her lip and starts to slowly get up. I watch, my eyebrows pinched, as she starts to get up and get dressed.

"Taylor, what's going on?"

Her shoulders slump, and she looks at her door before sitting next to me on her bed again, "I just feel bad. Like I'm flaunting my relationships, or something, in front of her sometimes. Kali is the best person ever, and I think she's looking for love while I sit here with three guys who make me feel special every day."

I brush the hair from her face and watch as a tear slides down her cheek. "That's not your fault. Listen, you can't make everyone else's problems yours. Kali will find love. Life's shitty at times, but it gets better. You just have to have faith or hope that it will get better." My words of comfort don't seem to be hitting their mark. Taylor doesn't look like she feels any less guilty for having a relationship with me. I know Kali is a touchy area. I don't want to hurt her either, she's cool. That doesn't mean I'm going to deny what Taylor and I have either. "Hey. Come on. What can I do to make it better? I don't like seeing you sad."

"Can we stay at the house tonight?" she asks, her doe-like eyes pinning me with her stare. There's no way I could deny her anything.

"Yeah, baby, that's fine," I reassure her and get up, starting to get dressed again. On our way out, I take her hand and lead her over to my car. Our ride is comfortable, and all the uncertainty and anxiousness to make her mine has ebbed some. I'm thankful for this opportunity, and I'll be hers for as long as she wants me.

When we pull up to the house and get out of the car, Taylor's hand grabs onto mine, and I like the way she doesn't shrink back from what this is. What we all want to give her while we make her ours, and keep her forever. We walk into the house, and the guys are still hovering around the table in the living room, looking over Jose's computers.

Steffan glances up first, his eyes darting to our girl first, before sliding over to me, and then back to her with a smile. "Hey, gorgeous," he drawls and holds an arm out to wrap her in. She goes willingly into his arms and gives him a hug.

"Should you be up and moving around already?" He glances down at her, and I see my best friend's tough exterior melt for her.

"I'm fine, little mouse," He assures her and drops a kiss to her forehead.

Soren glances up, and his glacial eyes cut me, "You weren't gone very long."

I roll my eyes at his insinuation, and move further into the room, choosing not to engage his crazy side. I know this new dynamic will be the hardest for Soren. He feels the most, even though you'd never know it. "Do we have anything yet?"

"Not yet," Steffan answers while Jose is practically glaring at the screen. His phone vibrates once, and he gets up to answer it.

"What are you looking for?" Taylor leans closer and asks.

"A missing child," Soren answers. My gaze shoots up and collides with Steffan's. Fucking Soren never thinks before he speaks. Taylor's face pales, and she looks like she could cry all over again. I'm about to argue when Jose moves to the front of the room, his phone in his hands.

"Ah, we have a problem," His face is focused, but I see a true ripple of concern in his eyes.

"What?" Steffan moves out of the tight circle and over to him reaching for his phone.

"The guys did a perimeter check, and they found a body close to the lake."

"No, shit," Soren grunts and throws down the papers he was holding. "Whose is it?"

"It's not human," Jose breathes out, his eyes darting around the room. I feel my stomach start to coil. "It's an alligator."

CHAPTER SEVENTEEN

Soren

This can't be real. The large, dark body lying on the grassy area away from the water is covered in blood. A few of our guys stand around it, heads bowed respectfully, and the sight of it all makes my gut clench. This can't happen. She wouldn't leave this way. Why is she so far from the water?

After Jose gave us the message, we secured the house, and the four of us left to investigate. Taylor stayed behind to keep overseeing our other project. I didn't need her witnessing the next greatest loss of my life if Jose's information was correct.

"We didn't touch anything, boss." One of the guys speaks to my brother, and Steffan nods at him. They keep moving closer to look, and I can't move. The way the dark body lies feels unnatural. This murder was gruesome, and this beast put up a fight.

"You saw no one on the cameras?" Lee questions

them, and all I can do is stand there feeling like my insides are crushing in.

Allison. The perfect beast of the water. Our other girl. The Ali that no one ever expects, the one who holds our secrets. We can't lose her. *I* can't lose her.

"No one, sir. We didn't hear a splash or a vehicle, nothing. After our first round, we came back, and the body was here."

Steffan moves closer, and every other footstep his eyes jump to me. I manage to keep my face closed off, refusing to let anyone know how much this is messing me up in the head. Only one other person knew how important Allison was to me, and I fed her his body last year when he was taken out. How the hell anyone knows about her now is a mystery.

"This isn't even what we've been seeing so far." Lee finally reacts to the damage in front of us.

"No wings, no snakes, just blood. Lots of carnage," Steffan huffs and rounds the gator. This is it. The part I want nothing to do with, but at the same time, I can't help but need it to be me.

"I'll look," I tell him, and he steps back with his head bowed. I hesitate before reaching for the massive jaw and jugular, turning the head to the side, refusing to glance into its golden, dead eyes that are staring at me. There is no mark.

"It's not her." I breathe out a sigh of relief and fall to the ground, my hands on my knees. Thank fuck it's not her.

"I don't get it then." Steffan shakes his head. "This clearly was an attack. The fight, the struggle, it's messy. If this isn't our usual killer, then what is happening."

The night replays in my head up until the minute Jose came into the room and showed us the text. All hell broke loose. Everyone scattered. Some went to the lake, the perimeter, only a few stayed at home to protect our most precious girl. Little mouse.

Little mouse!

"It's not an attack on the alligator, it's a diversion. They knew we'd come. Fuck! We left Taylor at the house." The words tumble out of my mouth, and my heart seizes.

Steffan and Lee bolt with me back to the cars. We messed up. We let all our attention go to this attack, and the news brought us here instead of staying with her. Whoever did this knew we'd come, that this would be too great a temptation for us not to be here. It was deliberate, a way to gain attention here, so we wouldn't focus on the house. We dropped our guard thinking the danger was out at the lake.

The drive feels like it takes forever even as Steffan breaks every law to get there. My hands are fisted in my lap, while Lee's knuckles are white as they grasp the barrel of his gun. I hope the killer is still there. Please let this be the night. It's time for the games to end. I could go for some blood. The possibility that this could finally be it has me unable to stay still. The pain I'd felt in my gut thinking they killed Allison... The anxiety and deep dread I have now with another attack on Taylor...

Oh they will bleed for this. These fuckers are going to suffer.

"Why are you smiling like that?" Lee asks me.

I glance at my brother and he just shakes his head. Good. We're on the same fucking page. He knows I'm about to lose my shit, and there's nothing anyone can do to stop me. These assholes won't stand a chance once I get within reach of them.

"I'm going to rip these fuckers to shreds. I'll make all their little stunts look like elementary level craft projects." I tell him and then look down at my hands that are vibrating from my rage.

"This isn't good," Lee's eyes widen, and I lift my head to look. The house is there, but the windows are completely black.

Little mouse better be safe. I'll torch this entire fucking town just to ensure I get the killer. Steffan throws the car in park, and we jump out. The rest of our guys are not too far behind. And that's when I hear it. Screaming. Blood curdling screams of someone being tortured.

I bolt to the door and twist the knob, but nothing gives. "It's locked."

Steffan bangs and yells while the screams keep going over and over again. I feel my stomach bottom out. If she's hurt, none of us will ever forgive ourselves. I won't be able to live without her anymore. An angry roar rips through my throat.

"Let me." Lee grunts and kicks the door in. Wood flies as the door shatters.

The emptiness in the house is eerie, only the monitor screens on the computers glow. I walk over to the little black box on the table with the letter attached to it. Steffan moves around me and flies up the stairs yelling for Taylor. I flip the switch on the box, and the screams stop. "It's a fucking recording."

"A little too real," Lee shakes his head.

A door slams, and there's yelling, but soon our guys are coming downstairs followed by Steffan and a brother who is cradling our girl in his arms. She's crying and clutching his shirt. I move to them, my gaze deadly on all the brothers that filed downstairs as well.

"What the hell happened?" Jose and Lee are bent over the black box, and I hand them the letter that was there.

"The lights went out," one of the brothers, another Scab who will be going through initiation soon, steps forward. "I grabbed Taylor and brought her upstairs."

"Someone was banging on the front door, and Preby and Nixon ran outside to see what was happening," another kid steps forward.

"We wanted to make sure to protect Taylor, so the rest of us headed upstairs. The lights were going crazy, and then all the screaming started. We didn't dare move until you guys came back."

I'm fucking pissed but also thankful as hell that their first priority was to protect Taylor. As it should always be. What we should have done. She's shaking in my brother's arms, her complexion pale, and her eyes are squeezed shut. She's mumbling against his chest, but I can't make out what she is saying. She's terrified, and the sight of it makes my chest squeeze in agony.

"What does the letter say?" I ask Lee without taking my eyes off Taylor.

Lee shakes his head, his jaw rock solid. "Got ya."

"What the fuck," Steffan yells, and the noise startles Taylor.

"Bro, calm down." Jose motions and stalks over to the computers to pull up the footage of our security.

"We're not going to find anything," I warn him, shaking my head. "If they had any chance of being on camera, why would they leave the house with the monitors still working."

Jose starts typing anyway, and I exhale loudly, unable to watch his futile attempts. Lee is staring at the recording machine. "What's that look for?"

"It's the same kind of machine that was at the school." His eyes slide to my brother who tenses. It is the same person fucking with us that did when Taylor was attacked. The last time we left her alone.

Steffan must read my mind because his gaze snaps up to mine. "She can't be left alone anymore. Whoever did this is taunting us every time."

He glances over to the brothers who are still standing around, looking scared of what we'll do, and shaken by the incident. "You are all dismissed. If anyone remembers anything, though, or something else comes to mind, tell us. You and you," he points to two other brothers. "Go search the perimeter and see if you can find Preby and Nixon."

They're probably dead is what I want to say, but I hold it in. So far this killer hasn't exactly been merciful, especially not to the Brotherhood. The one holding Taylor looks confused. I narrow my eyes at him and clarify. "You stay. *Obviously.*" She's fucking terrified, was he thinking he was just going to drop her on the floor and leave?

I walk over to Jose and watch him flip through the footage. It's almost eerie to see the house movement and then everything goes black. The room clears out, and only then does Lee shift in closer to us. "Here." He hands me the paper, and I scan it.

"This says a lot more than 'Got ya' on it." I raise my brow, and he looks up the stairs where the last of the brothers are disappearing to. I read out loud.

Got ya.

Eye for an eye.

Skin for skin.

Blood for blood.

Collecting hearts is all in fun.

The Illicit will fall. Bathed in the blood of their mistakes.

"If the theory is that this is not the same killer, how do we know who this belongs to? People have died in too many ways to be able to tell, but this letter was one person," Jose breaks the silence. "And who is screaming on the recording?"

He hits a button on the screen, and I watch this time as just one figure barely blurs in the edge of the camera before the house goes dark. There's a bang. And within thirty seconds, the screaming starts. Taylor jumps in the brother's arms, her body goes rigid, and her mouth tips open in a scream.

CHAPTER EIGHTEEN

Taylor

The mask. It was the same person from the football field. They were wearing Soren's mask. The neon skull mask he'd been wearing when we first met, when I didn't know who he was yet. We had an instant connection, and I'd let him take my virginity. He still wears it sometimes when we make love. Now it's being used to terrify me – to haunt me. I'll never be able to look at him in that mask again. I don't think I can see *any* of the brothers in those masks again.

Never.

"Give her to me!" Soren growls. I feel his hands come on me, but they're too rough. They remind me too much of the monster in the mask. My head is moving back and forth as I try to bury myself deeper into the brother who came to rescue me from my room.

"Little mouse," Soren's voice softens. "Taylor. It's me."

"Go away," I cry. "I can't right now. Go away."

I feel the presence of someone else. Then I hear Lee. "Taylor?"

"No." I sniffle.

"Mouse?" Steffan tries to reach for me.

"I-I can't look at any of you right now."

"Why?" Steffan's voice remains level and calm. "What happened?"

"They wore your mask again. And I'm afraid when I look at you, I'll see them." I can feel the weight of my words on them. The silence is heavy between us. As much as I want to turn around and take them in my arms, I can't. My mental health isn't stable enough at the moment.

"This fucker," Soren mumbles. I hear wood being broken and then glass shattering.

"That's *not* helping. She's in shock and just went through a traumatic experience," Lee tells him.

Steffan's soothing voice asks, "Are you hurt?"

"No. But someone is."

"Who?"

"I don't know. I heard screaming. But I was too scared to leave my room." I can't stop my tears of shame. "They came for me anyway. The door was kicked open and I saw the bloody knife... they placed a snake on the floor... I screamed...then the sound of people coming startled them, and they ran to the window and climbed out."

The brother holding me tightens his grip. I want so badly for it to be one of my boys, but I can't right now. The sight of the snake reminded me of the time I walked out into the yard, and Soren held a black snake. At the time I thought it was Steffan. My brain is too scrambled. Memories and traumatic experiences are all blending together.

"Take her to her room," Steffan tells the brother holding me.

I jump at that. "No. I can't go back there."

Heavy footfalls approach. Then I hear Soren. "I've removed every single mask."

I look and there's Soren with a few of the brothers carrying a box full of discarded masks.

"That's not enough," Lee tells him. "Let's take her to Blue Rose fifty-four."

I'm not sure what that's code for, but the twins seem to agree with him. The brothers that came with Soren ask what the code means.

"If we wanted you to know where we were taking her, we wouldn't have used a code," Soren tells them.

Steffan, ever the peacemaker, adds, "The fewer people who know, the better. It's to keep her safe and not put anyone else at risk."

"President Carmichael," a voice from above calls out. "We found another body. Possibly the one who had been screaming."

"Who is it?"

"Kali, sir."

I wiggle free, and as soon as my feet hit the floor, I take off in a hard run. "Kali! Kali! Kali!" I climb the stairs, taking two steps at a time. "*Kali!*"

If my best friend—no. I won't survive this loss. The thought that while I was crying and being a coward, she was struggling for her life has my chest caving in.

"I have to go to her. I want to see her."

"No," Soren tells me firmly. He may want to protect me, but I have to see my friend. I've seen multiple deaths, more than any person should, and on a college campus of all places. I narrow my eyes at him, and he releases a heavy sigh. "At least let me go check first?"

"Thank you."

When he reaches out to touch me, I take a step back. Seeing the killer wear their masks has me on edge still. "When you're ready, let me be here for you." And then he turns around and hurries up the stairs.

Lee and Steffan don't crowd me, but they remain close. I keep my eyes trained on the stairs as I wait for Soren's return.

They said they found a body—not a dead body. There's hope. I have to maintain hope, no matter how far-fetched or foolish it may seem.

Heavy footfalls are coming from above. Soren appears at the top of the landing. "It's not her. Bloody boot prints lead to the window. We need to circle and see if we can track them."

Though I hate that this other girl lost her life, especially so young, I find relief in that it wasn't Kali. I take out my cell and call her. Extremely inappropriate music lyrics begin in the distance. They stop, and begin again.

"It's coming from the door that leads to the sanctuary." Lee turns and hurries toward the faint sound of Kali's ringtone for me.

Her voicemail picks up so I quickly end the call and try again. I follow the guys as the phone rings in my ears.

I've never gone to this area. I'm typically not allowed here, but the guys are more focused on finding

Kali's phone. As we turn around the corner, there's a glow coming from a dark corner on the floor. Steffan flips a light switch to reveal two large wooden doors with elegant carvings and trimmings around them. Above them is a metal Delta Pi Theta crest. There in the corner is a body with wild red hair and ghostly white skin, blue jean shorts with dark splatters, and a ripped, pink, silk shirt. Her hair is covering her face, but I already know who it is.

"Kali!" I cry and rush to her before anyone can stop me. Her skin is cold as I gently brush her tangled locks from her face. "She's breathing!" A river of tears streams down my face.

"She's breathing! Oh thank God, she's breathing! Call 9-1-1."

Nobody moves so I yell again, "Call 9-1-1. Steffan, please."

"We'll call our doctor, and our guy on the force. We're not going to have the entire police department here."

He can't be serious. But he is. I pull Kali into my arms. "I'm so sorry I got you involved in all this," I whimper into her hair. Everyone around me dies. She was kind and befriended me. A breath of fresh air compared to all the people in my life before.

"Don't get snot on me."

Her voice is weak, but I've never heard anything so wonderful. "Kali! Thank God you're alive."

"I think he'd rather y'all have to deal with me than Him. I'm such a pain in the ass that even Satan himself won't take me." How she can joke right now, is beyond me.

Soren gives a halfhearted chuckle at her comment. "That actually checks out."

"Would explain how you're still alive," Lee mumbles about Soren.

Succo nods in agreement. "And Steffan."

"Steffan isn't *that* bad," Lee teases. "But if they took Steffan, his dark, psychotic shadow would come, too. That's just more trouble than it's worth."

Soren pulls out a cigarette and lights it. "Let that be a warning to you fuckers. Even Hell fears me coming through their gates."

Lee and Succo don't comment. Soren offers a small smirk, but his eyes are piercing and show no sign of humor. I clear my throat because we still have a dead body and half dead Kali. "My friend needs help."

Soren crouches down and blows smoke out of the side of his lips. "Do you have any useful information?"

Kali blinks at him and then smiles. "I know things you could only dream of knowing."

"Cute. Remind me again why I should waste resources on you?"

"Soren," I scold. I hold my friend closer. "You don't have to tell us anything if you don't have the energy."

"Sure. We can wait and see how many more bodies pile up. Maybe the killer will start leaving them like breadcrumbs so that we can follow the trail."

Kali snorts. "You're even creepier when you try to joke."

The doorbell chimes, and Succo holds a finger up. "I'll get it."

The doctor and police officer take Kali to the hospital. Steffan charges Lee and Succo with helping me pack while he and Soren make preparations to transport me to one of their secret houses.

CHAPTER NINETEEN

Steffan

Soren and I gather the brothers for an emergency meeting. We'd concluded that Kali had barely escaped the killer, and we found her by the door because it was locked, and she'd most likely lost the energy to keep going, so she hid in the corner. Soren and I divide the brothers and give our instructions. We also put someone else in charge of the scabs since Lee is going to be away.

"Think Amir Concord is responsible?" Soren asks after everyone has been dismissed.

"No," I tell him. We both begin heading up the marble steps out of the sanctuary as I continue speaking. "This isn't Amir. He shot his trophy wife in cold blood while she was standing a hair away from his golden boy. That man isn't going to waste his time with college students. No, this is our original killer. Snakes were found. A knife was used on the victims. They keep switching a few things up on us, but there's still a common theme."

Soren holds the door open as I pass through. "But who is left that could be behind this?"

One would think all the deaths would narrow the list down; however, that doesn't seem to be the case. "Every time we dig, we uncover more secrets."

"So we keep digging."

I nod. "We keep digging." We enter the giant foyer and stop. "Go pack. We have much to do."

Taylor should be safe on the Alabama coast. Very few within The Illicit know of that house for situations like this, a betrayal from within. I'm more convinced than ever that someone from The Illicit is out for either revenge or power. Whatever the case, they're out for blood. This runs deeper than the petty dispute between the Van Dorens, which we had originally and foolishly assumed it was all over. More than the last of Dupree's family line turning on him. Then there's the bastard child of Amir Concord. What do they have to gain from all this? Possibly Amir and the child are working together to overthrow the top ranking families. I wouldn't have thought Amir would torture his own daughter, but he did shoot his wife to protect the name of his child.

I go back to what I told Soren before. Amir wouldn't waste his time, energy, and resources on the death of a bunch of college students. Those murders would be considered meaningless and beneath him.

Taylor's roommate at the beginning of the year was murdered, and now her current roommate was attacked. Who is connected to Taylor *and* The Illicit. She comes from a middle-class family in the middle of nowhere and was raised in a borderline religious cult. Her ex-boyfriend was a direct descendant of Walter Dupree, but Walter killed Alex. It doesn't make sense. Yet fate has crossed our paths, and we're all somehow connected to this killer.

Who is the missing link?

Soren drives like a possessed lunatic. Wait—he is a possessed lunatic. I love my twin more than anything, or anyone, but he definitely has his issues. Then again, that's part of his charm. Regardless, I silently say a prayer that we'll arrive alive and soon.

We drive around the winding roads as if we're competing in a Formula One race. My father was a ruthless criminal, cold and calculated. I grew up in The Illicit, surrounded by people who would slit your throat with a smile. I negotiate with some of the most dangerous people in the world – I don't scare easily . Right now, my asscheeks are clenched and I'm clutching onto anything I can find in the interior of this Jeep.

Through gritted teeth I complain. "I should've agreed to take the motorcycles."

Soren, who thrives off life-threatening situations, of course laughs. "Have you pissed yourself?"

"No. I knew better than to drink anything before getting in a car with you behind the wheel."

The vehicle fishtails around a curve but Soren quickly straightens the wheel, and then the engine roars as he continues to drive far over the speed limit. "Sorry, bro. I'm just ready to get to our little mouse. I have this feeling that something bad is about to happen."

I frown, because his driving is tempting death at the moment. It's nighttime and we can barely see the narrow road. Instead of arguing logic with my brother, I humor him. "Bad shit is always happening. Did you finally start giving a shit?" I can't help but tease him, so I say, "Fuck me. Soren, has Taylor made you go soft?"

"I'm never soft when it comes to her. In fact, my dick keeps hitting the steering wheel. I even raised it up as high as it'll go. Motherfucker sitting over here going booii-ooiing every time I make a turn."

"You're so full of shit."

"There's our turn. Ready? Watch."

I refuse to look at my brother's dick hitting the steering wheel—which I doubt is even happening. *Idiot.* I do share his excitement on arriving at the beach house. One, I'm ready to get out of this death trap and allow my stomach to settle. Two, I need to see with my own eyes that Taylor is safe.

The large, raised, blue house with white shutters comes into view. Our Jeep bounces on the gravel road.

"Think Lee touched her while we were gone?" He sounds casual, but I know he's biding his time . It'll only take one time for Lee to fuck up, and Soren will be right there waiting and ready.

"Soren, don't do anything."

"I'm going to do plenty when I get in there. But if he touched her without one of us, then I'll do plenty to him... with a knife."

A knife? Sounds threatening, but I know that's one of Soren's kinks. Maybe he is warming up to the idea of Lee. "Wouldn't you enjoy that?" I tell him in a smug tone.

Soren shoves the Jeep into park. "I'm not the one wanting to fuck him. But if you want, I'll let you watch, and then you can use his blood as lube."

"You're a sick fuck."

"You're sharing your girlfriend with your handsome twin, and best friend—whom you also want to fuck. Let's not judge, eh?" Soren opens his door and then slams it shut. I hurry and do the same because he does not need to walk in there alone. He looks at me with one of his rare genuine smiles. "We're cut from the same cloth, brother."

He always sees right through me. My twin knows me better than anyone. Tonight, I do plan to fuck Taylor, and Lee.

CHAPTER TWENTY

Lee

Typically, I refuse to drink coffee at night, but I need it. My adrenaline from earlier is starting to crash. I stare out the window above the kitchen sink at the moon's reflection dancing over the water. Taylor is safe upstairs with Succo. A part of me wishes that we'd be staying here for a while. A mini vacation away from all the chaos would be a fucking dream. Footsteps sound on the front porch. I hear Soren's voice so I don't panic.

Soren and Steffan enter the house with their eyes already seeking out Taylor. No "hello," or "fuck you," nothing. They look around, and then at me, expectantly. "She's upstairs taking a bath. Succo is guarding the door."

"From you?" Soren asks. His cold eyes are challenging me to cower down to him, or dare to get angry with him.

And here we go... At least we all had a little moment of peace-. I know Soren has had it rough. He was raised by Rhett Carmichael. Trained to be a ruthless killer from his grade school years. Sent away by his family. But I honestly believe even if all that hadn't happened, he would still be a major dick. Some people are just born assholes. Soren Carmichael is one of those people.

He's waiting for my answer as I take a leisurely sip of my coffee. I meet his hard gaze and calmly tell him. "No. From you." I place the cup in the sink and then cross my arms. "I figured you'd be ready to pounce, and she needs to have some time for herself."

Soren scoffs. "And you think your little pet could keep me out? Adorable."

Of course Taylor isn't being guarded from Soren, but he's too much of a dick not to fuck with. He walks off, and I'm grateful that Steffan and I are finally alone together. We haven't addressed what's going on between us. Are we simply sharing Taylor and enjoying each other's pleasure...or is there something between him and me as well?

Steffan slowly approaches me. He drops the duffel he is holding and then takes my face between his large hands. "I'm glad you're okay. Thank you for seeing to our girl."

I grip his strong wrists as I take a hard swallow. "You're the one who just recovered. Glad to see you made it back. No more incidents, I hope?"

"No. And frankly, I don't want to talk about the Brotherhood, families, or The Illicit. I don't want to talk at all."

My eyes zero in on his perfectly shaped lips. Soren and Steffan are identical twins, yet Steffan has always been the more attractive one to me. It's insane how they physically look the same, but they carry themselves in such opposite manners , it makes it easy to tell them apart. Soren is rough. His sharp jawline could cut glass, whereas Steffan is the exact same, but his reminds me of a runway model. Soren's blond hair is always wet, or greasy looking, from the gel he uses. Steffan's hair is full of body and seems to always fall naturally into place. Both have stunning blue eyes. Soren's eyes are like a raging storm. Ones that stare into your soul. Steffan's are peaceful waters, so soothing and kind that you want to get lost in them. Soren is a handsome villain, and his looks are his weapon of pure evil. Steffan is a legend, god, or king, with so much power and grace, coming to save the day at any cost, and his royal features are a bonus. When he conquers his enemies, he does it with more class and less chaos.

It hits me like a ton of bricks. I've been obsessing over him for years. Sure, I've always found him attractive, but I can tell you every detail about him. Not only his physical features, but I know him almost as well as myself. Yet I have not the slightest clue where I stand with him. I pull back, and free myself from his grip. Rubbing the back of my neck, I look up to the ceiling. "Steff. We have to talk, man."

"We're safe here."

"We're never fucking safe in this world, and you know that. But that's not what I meant." I face the man whom I've grown up with. The one person in this world I truly respect and admire. He's been my brother and best friend forever. "Tell me what's going on between us?"

"If I have to tell you, then I guess nothing." He looks pissed, but fuck him. He's going to talk about this. He's going to tell me exactly where I stand with him.

"I know how I feel. I know how I feel when I'm with you, and how I feel when I'm not. I know how I feel the chemistry that's always been there, but over the years has matured into so much. Steffan," my voice pleading for him to hear what I'm trying to tell him, "I'm not a mind reader. I want full transparency, so there's no misunderstandings. I only know how I feel, and I can't possibly know what you're feeling unless you tell me."

Steffan approaches me again. His eyes have darkened. Everyone labels Soren as the more dangerous twin, but that's only because he's more unpredictable. Steffan is equally as dangerous and as much of a predator. He's more calculated and knows how to keep his cool. Right now I'm getting to see that side. Those piercing blue eyes have zeroed in on me, and each step forward is deliberate and slow.

"Okay, Lee." His tone is cool with an edge. "I've spent years wanting to have my cum dripping from those full pouty lips of yours. To have you reek of me." He circles me like a hungry wolf. "That beautiful, perfect hair of yours? I want to sink my fingers into it and grip it so your scalp feels the sting, all while I hold you down and fuck you in the ass. Then, I'd blow my load all over you." When he gets back to standing in front of me, he reaches between my legs and cups me. "I want this dick in my mouth. I want to taste you at the back of my throat. Then I'd spit your cum into Taylor's mouth. I'd watch you fuck her, and then I'd use your cum as lube for when I fuck her, while my twin watches." He grips my dick. "Does that get you hard, Prince Concord?"

"Don't fucking call me that," I say through gritted teeth. I hate how everyone refers to me as the 'prince.' We're not royalty. A few people might see my family that way. Steffan knows it. He's trying to rile me up. And fuck me, if it isn't working.

"Full transparency—you're mine. And when my dick is inside you, I'll call you whatever I want."

"But your dick isn't inside me right now. So don't. Call. Me. That."

Steffan's hand is lightning fast as it grabs me by the throat. "We can change that, m*y little prince*."

I can't stop myself. His forcefulness. Calling me that. My orgasm hits me so fast that I'm unprepared. Steffan rubs my cock over my pants and smiles when he feels the wetness coming through. Before I can explain myself, he grips my chin and kisses me. His hot tongue snakes through and claims mine. I moan into him. Slowly, the kiss calms, and he becomes more gentle. He's telling me everything I need to know. Full transparency. This isn't lust. This isn't some short term arrangement to get his rocks off.

I'm Steffan Carmichael's little prince.

After I clean up, I meet Jose in the hallway. "Are you leaving?"

Jose smiles. "Yeah. Now that Taylor has Steffan and Soren, I'm going to go relocate Chanda. And stay with her."

"I appreciate you protecting my sister." And I mean it. After her being married to that piece of garbage, I appreciate Succo being there for her. Really wish he hadn't kept it from me for so long, but I get it. I walk Brother Succo to the door and lock it behind him.

We're alone. The twins. Taylor. And me.

I walk over to the patio door and stare out into the ocean. The sound of the waves instantly calms my nerves. I slide the door open and step out onto the wooden deck. I slide my socks off. The wood is cool beneath my feet as I walk off the deck and into the sand. Collapsing onto the shore, I allow my feet to sink into the wet sand and let the waves crash against me, even though I'm still fully clothed.

Fuck. What's happening in my life right now. High school years were spent as a rich, spoiled playboy. I literally had my choice of anyone. I could do anything, and get away with it. My family was picture-perfect, even in my eyes. Life was simple.

College has been hell. Fucking hell. This is supposed to be the best years of my life. I'm supposed to be learning and growing, to take my place as a leader in The Illicit. No more a prince, but I'm ready to take kingdom status. When I was younger, I thought the men of The Illicit were gods. But I feel lost. Confused. Scared. For the longest time, depressed. I thought I'd found my person, but then she was ripped from me. My perfect family. I went from loving and respecting my father to witnessing him murder my mother, and now despising him. It's hard because I miss him, yet I want to peel the skin from his bones for killing the woman who gave me life and raised me.

Now I've crossed into new territory with my best friend. I love Steffan. I love Taylor. I tolerate Soren. What if all this goes sideways? Taylor has become a valuable friend as well. I've lost so much family. I'm terrified of losing them. If they were murdered, I'm not sure I'd recover. What if I lose them because this polyamorous relationship doesn't work? That'd be worse than death. I'd feel responsible because I was the outsider. She originally chose Steffan and Soren. She was theirs. I knew that. And maybe I should've kept it all about sharing Taylor. I've made it clear that Steffan can bring me to my knees by barely touching me. The lines are no longer blurred, but they've been crossed. We're no longer dancing on the edge, we've jumped. I only pray that I haven't screwed my life up worse. That I might've let my desires and urges ruin the only family I have remaining.

"What are you doing out here by yourself?" I look up to see Taylor's sweet face glowing from the lights shining behind her. She's wearing a plain white dress that touches her ankles and flows easily in the breeze. An angel who has come out here to pull me out of the darkness.

I lean back on my elbows as a wave comes up and douses my chest. "I'm debating if I want to float off. Just let the waves carry me away."

She rolls her eyes at me and shakes her head with a light giggle. "In those dark waters? Not concerned about sharks?"

I look at her out of the corner of my eye. "I live with an alligator in my backyard."

"He's used to swimming with sharks," Steffan calls out as he and Soren walk through the sand to join us.

"Those are a different type of shark. These are actual sharks," Taylor argues.

Soren plops down with a splash and pulls Taylor down with him. "Out here wallowing in self-loathing, Concord?"

"I might risk the dangers just not to have to listen to you," I mumble to myself.

Soren hears me and says, "I'd be more than happy to give you a push out."

"You two stop." Taylor dips her hand in the water and then flicks the droplets at Soren's face. It's fucking weird to see anyone be playful with him. If I flicked water in his face, he'd hold my head under water until I quit blowing bubbles.

"I agree. You two are worse than children," Steffan scolds.

Soren cups some water in his hand and then trickles it down Taylor's chest. The white becomes see-through showing off the curve of her ample cleavage. "Does that make you the mommy in this relationship?"

Taylor vehemently shakes her head. "No. We're not doing that."

"Really? That's where you're going to draw the line?"

"Yes. I don't want you calling me your mommy."

"You know I do love to cross lines."

"Soren. Please. Not this one. Not yet." Taylor's face turns sad and I hear her whisper, "Lee just lost his mother."

Shockingly enough, Soren actually looks somewhat remorseful. If that sympathy is geared to me, or Taylor's bleeding heart, I am unsure.

We take a moment to all sit and enjoy the water cascading over our legs. The breeze keeps us cool. The quietness surrounding us. Not speaking a word, Steffan stands up and begins to undress. Soren raises Taylor up enough to slide out from under her. He follows his brother's cue. Taylor rises to her knees, but before she can fully stand, Soren slowly shakes his head at her. I follow their lead and stand up to remove my clothing.

When I turn to look at Taylor, I know exactly why Soren told her to not move. She looks like a siren. Her hair is partially damp hanging down to her shoulders. The white dress, that dry would look like pure virginal angel, now damp clings to her sinful body. This woman would lure any man to his death. Her sweet nature and effortlessly seductive appearance has my heart pounding in my chest, my knees are physically trembling, and all the blood has traveled south as my dick is throbbing—*begging* to be inside of her.

"Are you ready for all three of us?" Steffan asks Taylor. His voice is so deep, and the way it rumbles, it forces my eyes to close as a shiver runs through me. I'm excited and nervous. I really hope I'm not fucking up. Taking a deep breath, I open my eyes to stare at our beautiful angel. All three of us stand before her, fully nude, waiting with bated breath for her answer.

"Yes."

Her confidence in her answer has wiped away any doubt and my insecurity. This feels right. I know with Taylor, Steffan, and yes, even Soren, I can win any fucking war against The Illicit, a serial killer, and even the war within myself.

She's ready, and so are *we*.

CHAPTER TWENTY-ONE

Taylor

"I want all of you," I tell them. "I'm more than ready." The water laps against my skin as I let my legs sink into the sand. Soren is already fisting himself as he wades through the shallow water to me.

I feel so confident and sexy kneeling before them in the night out in the open. Soren is on my left. Lee in the center. Steffan is on the right. It's empowering having these three men looking at me with such desire and adoration.

"You're hot as fuck, but you're more than that. You are so special, Taylor." Lee speaks to me as if he's confessing a secret. Maybe he's wanted this longer than I imagined.

"Wait until you taste just how special she is," Steffan's husky voice has me fisting my dress.

"Fuck yes. I want your pussy, Taylor." Lee pleads as his chest rises and falls.

"Are you hungry for his dick, little mouse?" Soren asks. I can't help but shrink a little under his gaze. I know he doesn't care much for Lee. His dark chuckles give me tingles of fear, excitement, and suspense. "It's okay if you do. I see your nipples hardening. I bet your pussy is so fucking wet that you've got a river streaming into the ocean."

"I want it to stream into my face," Steffan tells me.

My voice has turned raspy as I try to speak over the lump in my throat. I'm so worked up. "Prove it. Instead of you three standing there talking while my skin shrivels like a prune."

"You're talking a big game for someone who can't keep their voice steady. Are you nervous?" Steffan arches a brow at me. There's three big cocks staring me in the face, I'd have to be delusional not to be a little nervous. The anticipation of where they're planning to shove those is both thrilling, and daunting.

"Tell you what, little mouse." Soren's eyes are breathtaking in the moonlight. They're dancing with mischief. "I'm going to give you a five minute head start. Wherever we catch you, is where we'll fuck you. And whoever catches you first, gets first dibs on which hole." His smile is pure wickedness.

"Why not here and now?" Lee asks. His twitching dick, and the painful longing in his eyes reveals how impatient he is right now.

"Because I don't want it to feel like rubbing sandpaper against my dick and having salt and sand in my ass the whole time. Have you never had sex on the beach? In salt water?" When Lee shrugs, Soren rolls his eyes and tells me, "Tick-tock, little mouse. Scurry along."

I love this idea. My face hurts from the smile that spreads across my face. I slide my wet, and now heavy, dress off so I can go faster and get out of the water easier. The sound of the three of them hissing only fuels my excitement. My feet slide and dip in the sand but I don't lose my balance.

Where should I go? I hurry into the house and head for the walk-in shower. I rinse the salt and sand from my body as fast as possible. I don't even wait for the water to warm. Goosebumps cover me as I run out still wet. I decide to wait for them at the first random bedroom door I come to upstairs. I leave the door open a crack and then go hide under the bed. The lights are off and it's so quiet my breathing sounds loud, like I'm wearing a Darth Vader mask.

The door downstairs opens and loudly slams shut. My heart rate accelerates with every heavy footfall. Lust hitting me down to my bones. If I'm not careful, I'll accidentally moan with excitement and give myself away. I'm shaking for them. Desperate for all three men.

"Little mouse. Come out, come out." Steffan calls as he continues past the door and down the hall.

Lee approaches the door, I know it's him by the sound of his voice. I watch his feet from under the bed go to the closet. "Come out, my sweet Taylor. I plan to take my time. My appetite is craving every part of you, and I am going to savor each touch and taste."

He walks out and I wait for Soren. Except after a few seconds, I feel two strong hands on my ankles. I yelp as I'm yanked from under the bed. My body is flipped to where I'm lying on my back, and a very nude and hard Soren is straddling me. "Gotcha."

"Where were you hiding? When did you sneak in?"

"Sshhh." He places his finger over my lips. He leans down, and his nose tickles at the tender skin between my legs. His deep inhale has me blushing. "Now. You're going to be quiet while I enjoy licking this pussy until you come so hard your thighs are twitching for hours later."

I've been waiting and needing one of them to find me. Of course it was Soren. Now that he's here, my desperation is taking over. He flicks his tongue over my clit, and I can't help myself. I grab his hair and shove his face harder between my legs. Soren growls against me, and the vibration has me getting shamelessly wet.

"Soren. Yes. Eat me alive. God." I'm about to come already. He begins sucking my clit sending all the tingles needed to have my legs twitching like he'd promised. "I need your tongue inside of me. Yes."

"Give me your cum . It's mine. I want it."

"Keep doing that, and I just might." I pant.

"Greedy prick." Steffan comes charging in and quickly drops beside us on the floor.

"Let's get her on the bed," Lee suggests while standing on the other side.

One final thrust with his tongue, Soren releases his hold on me. "Alright. Tell us where you want us."

Soren helps me stand and climb up on the bed. I take a moment to think about it. Steffan and Lee both rubbing against me and each other sounds delicious. While Soren savagely fucks my mouth...

"*Fuck.*"

I guess I was mumbling that out loud. Before I can even take my next breath, the men waste not another second making my fantasy a reality. But instead of Steffan and Lee entering me at the same time, Lee enters my pussy painfully slowly, stretching me. Our eyes collide and so do our hearts. I'm grateful that the twins are allowing us a moment to just be us, before it becomes all of us.

Lee brings me to my knees and slides behind me. He pumps into me from behind holding me against him, my back to his chest. Steffan climbs on the bed to join us. He uses two fingers to spread my lips further apart as he licks my clit. Over and over. But then he eases deeper in. Licking not only my clit, but also Lee's shaft. The idea he is tasting both of us has me trembling in Lee's hold.

"You're making me light-headed." I pant.

Soren comes into view. "Do I want to fuck these tits or your mouth? What do you think?"

"I can't think right now. Both? Both. Why choose, right?"

"That's my girl." Soren says through a devilious smile.

He begins sucking my nipple while his hand thrills the other with massaging and pinching.

"Yes," I sigh. I place my hands on Steffan's strong shoulders for support.

"You're mine." Soren nips my breast before placing a sensual kiss on it.

"And mine." Lee whispers into my ear.

"And mine." Steffan emphasizes his claim with a love bite on my thigh and long lick up to my pussy.

"I'm yours. You can all have me. Take me. Keep me."

Soren places both of his hands on my breasts. "As if we'd ever let you go."

"Or let anyone else have you," Steffan adds.

"Brother, I need you to slide over. I'm about to fuck these gorgeous tits." Soren spits on my chest and presses my breasts together. "Fucking stunning."

Lee continues pounding into me as Soren stands on the edge of the bed so his dick is level with my tits. He presses them together and begins fucking between them.

Steffan comes to my side and claims my mouth. Despite everything that's happening, I still get lost in his kiss. He pulls away and says, "I can hear how wet you're getting. It makes my mouth water. I love it when that pussy glistens." He grips my throat. "You know what I love even more?"

"What?"

"Fucking that ass." He smiles at me and waits for my nod. I do, and he looks at Lee. "Can you provide me some lube?"

Lee pounds into me harder and then pushes me forward. Soren hops off the bed, and I am eye level with his dick. Instantly my mouth opens for him, and he fucks my mouth like a savage as Lee pulls out and comes all over my asshole. Steffan takes his two fingers and smears it around the puckered hole and his dick.

I grip the mattress as Steffan eases into me. Each push from behind forces me to take more of Soren into my mouth. Lee reaches between the two men and begins fingering my clit, and his other hand plays with Steffan's balls and backside. The sex can be smelled in the air. My body is glistening and wound so tightly. I'm so full and stimulated.

"I'm going... I'm ... " I try to speak around Soren's dick. Drool drips down from my jaw, and my eyes are watering.

"Not yet." Steffan demands.

I'm trying. Lord knows I'm trying. I'm so wet, and my clit is swollen. My whole body is vibrating. I've never felt this dirty... I love it. I love how they make me feel–not only sexually, but emotionally. Submitting to them. Owning them as much as they own me. These three dangerous men allow me so much control over them. It's intoxicating. But it's their souls. At the center of their little black criminal hearts are good souls.

Soren grunts. "I'm about to..."

"Wait." Steffan tells him. "Little mouse. Jack off Lee while you deepthroat my twin."

I'm not sure I'm coordinated enough to multitask sucking and jerking, especially from a side angle, but I'll do my best. Lee scoots until we're side to side. Soren leans over and spits on my hand, and then I use it to pump Lee.

"Don't worry. I'll handle your mouth, you focus on him." Soren must read my mind or feel my hesitation.

Before long I feel Lee's balls tightening. Steffan is becoming more animalistic behind me. Soren is about to physically choke me. And my vision is about to turn white from the orgasm that's building. Finally Steffan roars, "Now!"

I'm dizzy. There's cum everywhere, and my orgasm is blinding and feels never-ending. This is the most forbidden and exhilarating moment of my life. Three huge bodies wrap around me, and I allow my body to give in to the exhaustion.

Waking up wrapped in the arms of all the men I love for once doesn't cause me anxiety or emotional distress. They've proven to me over and over that no matter what, I am their top priority. I belong to them. They are mine. So when they had to leave to attend to their Illicit business I fell back asleep. The sounds of the ocean in the background add to the peace I feel. I don't even know how I can feel this taken care of when my best friend was almost killed. Kali was almost added to the category of the people we've lost, and mourn. If the guys had been any later, I'm not sure what would have happened to either of us. My mind still shrinks away from thinking of Chanda and her injuries.

The guys are convinced that all of these events are not connected, but I don't know if I believe it. Jose has been working nonstop to look into the past and find things about Lee's father's past, and I'm not sure that's the answer either. All I know is what has happened since school started, and the violence I've witnessed. Steffan won't say it, Lee can't think about it, but I know when

Soren looks into my eyes, he questions if these murders have anything to do with me. I am well aware, as I always have been, that some of the people closest to me are no longer with us. Except for Chanda and now Kali.

My mind is a mess of questions without answers. Having the guys here helps calm the fears I have, but when they're gone, I usually sink into self-doubt. After their claiming me last night, I no longer feel that way. I want to be strong for them. I need to be their constant while they rule the world they were born into.

With a new perspective on life, and not only wanting to take care of my men, but to be strong for myself, I decide I need to get up and start helping. I grab a shower and change into the jeans and university T-shirt that were packed for me, then head down to the main level for breakfast. I'm only slightly surprised to see the number of guards that are standing watch in the house. The way Steffan made it sound was that this house, or property, was secluded and was unknown to even the higher-ups of The Illicit. This is a place only the guys have access to.

After eating, I head to the office space where there is a detailed timeline of events laid out on the desk, and Jose's computer is still sifting through information while he is away. I glance at the screen and see that the count is well up over the hundreds. Hundreds of children who were born in the year that Lee's father supposedly got another woman pregnant. The other screen is focusing on blood and familial ties to the fifth family of The Illicit, which was made extinct.

I move to the timeline and work over all the details. I force myself to look at the image of Bryce's leg from the night of the Halloween party and try my hardest not to cry when I see Ava's school ID picture. I hate the small amount of jealousy I feel when I look at the homecoming queen's image and her timeline traced back to when Lee had some interest in her. Alex's picture is next, followed by the deaths of the football players, snakes, Bryce back on campus, Bailee's death, Rhett Carmichael's demise, the students who were found without hearts, Lois's death. And then all the other mass murders that were covered in the news, but never officially connected to the university, yet somehow are connected to The Illicit. The Angel Maker at the nursing home, and finally to Chanda's injuries and abduction. And now Kali is on the board.

The pictures and order of events tug at my heart and make it difficult to breathe. We've been fighting this battle for so long that sometimes I think the guys forget key pieces. The parts that include me. I take a picture and send it to Jose's computer then print it off on a sheet of paper. My hands shake while I place my image up there in the middle. Slowly, I start to draw lines to each event. I mark where I was. And in some instances, I make notes of my relationship to each person. Soon the web I've created has touched almost everyone. The realization makes my stomach clench. The sight makes me want to be sick.

"You don't think this is because of you, right?"

I whip around, and hurriedly rub the tears off my cheeks, right as Chanda walks over, her arms crossed over her chest while her eyes run over me. I haven't seen her since her attack. I take notice right away of the way her back is no longer hunched over in pain, but she's standing tall, proud, regal, like the queen of the Concord family she is.

"I think the evidence strongly supports my theory that even if I'm not the reason, I'm highly connected to it." My eyes flicker back over to the map.

Chanda's gaze moves over my handy work, "I used to think it was you. I thought there was no possible way all these people so close to Taylor were dying, and she wasn't involved. Then I saw the way Lee looked at you, and I panicked even more."

"And now?" I question, hating that my heart is racing so hard that she thought I could be capable of the destruction we've faced.

Her brow quirks, and a small smile touches her ruby-red lips. "I see the way you look at my brother. I see the way you are with the evil twin and Steffan. More than that I saw the devastation on your face when we found Lois. Then I was taken. It wasn't your voice that taunted me. I know it's not who you are, so you shouldn't let what is happening define you either."

"I'm sorry that it happened to you. I'll never forget how it felt thinking I would lose Steffan when he was hurt, either. I want them to see all the connections and not to be blind to what could be in front of them." I shrug and rub away more tears with my hands.

"It takes a lot more to break me. Believe it or not, but I'm not a stranger to death, or to abuse. I lived in fear most of my life until I learned to harness the demon that was created inside of me. Now I fight my own battles, but it's lonely. Even though...well even though

I'm working to share the burden, it is hard to relinquish the instinct to fight for your life." Her hand lands on my arm before she gives me a small hug. "These guys aren't blind to your connection to the events. They just don't want you to lose the loving warmth that makes you who you are. The reason they all love you."

I pull myself straighter at her words and let the glow of the love I feel from my guys surround me. "Are you okay with my love for Lee?"

Chanda laughs out loud, and her eyes gleam. "I'm living for this whole relationship. Not that I can handle another man or even two more, but I'm rooting for you all."

"Well that's good at least." I laugh with her, and we both look over the timelines. Chanda picks up the marker and makes a few connections to herself and also adds two important facts I wasn't aware of.

"You received texts?"

"Someone reached out to me. This"—she points to her back—"wasn't the first time I heard about blood or connection."

"Does Lee know?"

"He will now." She sits in one of the chairs, exhaustion rolling over her features. "Jose knows. I think it's time that we're all on the same page so we can work together without everyone fighting their own battles. When do they get back?"

"I have no idea. They don't exactly share all The Illicit business with me yet," I reply and join her in another chair.

"Stupid men. Always thinking women are weak and can't handle a little bloodshed."

I smirk and recline back. "What are your honest thoughts? One person? Two? What is their motive?"

Chanda bites her bottom lip and leans toward the images. I watch her closely, and I see the involuntary shiver that breaks out over her skin. "There were two people when I was taken. But only one person who controlled the narrative and created my injury. Motivation is even harder. Some of these are calculated and precise, while others appear more crimes of passion, or jealousy. The homecoming queen, the football players, your roommate, Lois, even Bailee's death, which we know Bryce was responsible for. Those killings seem more personal. The Angel Maker and the MC seem more impersonal, bigger, and more about The Illicit."

"Or distractions to the true motive." I turn to her. "Just like the other night. An alligator was killed just to lure the guys away because Allison is important to Soren, then the attack was made on the house. Which leads me back to the original theory that this is one person who uses and preys upon others, like your situation with Rhett, and Bryce's situation with Bailee, to get the outcome they want."

"But what is the purpose of the outcome?" Chanda laughs, but the noise is without joy. "To mess with us? To hurt someone?"

"It hurt you. Bailee's death hurt Lee."

Chanda leans in with a spark in her eye right before a notification on Jose's computer goes off. We both glance at the monitor where it's flashing red and reading the word MATCH.

I move from the table and collapse into the chair in front of the monitor. Clicking the mouse, I scan over the information. "Did you know that the nursing home used to be a hospital with a maternity ward?"

"No." Chanda shakes her head, her eyes widening. "Our families normally use C+C Hospital for births, especially heirs."

"A child was born there within the same birth year as Soren, Steffan, and Lee, about six months after them," I read, and I can feel my heartbeat in my temples.

"The date is a month before the fifth family was dismantled," Chanda breathes out and both of us glance at each other. "I'm texting Jose. The guys need to get back here right away."

CHAPTER TWENTY-TWO

Lee

For the first time ever, I glance at Steffan with annoyance. It's thanks to my oldest friend that we're standing here, in a dusty, abandoned building, instead of wrapped around our delicious and naked girlfriend. I glance at him from the corner of my eye and watch as he shifts, his specially tailored suit moving as a second skin with his body. To many, he looks calm, but I can see the irritation glaring under his skin. He's subtle about not wanting to be here, unlike Soren who is practically vibrating with resentment. Jose's phone pings nearby and he reaches into his pocket to read it. His brow furrows before he glances at me.

"The computer matched something. Chanda and Taylor want us to come back as soon as we can," he reports, and I nod my head at him.

"I vote we go now," Soren replies and moves to walk toward the back entrance where our car is parked.

"Stop. We're already here. Let's get this over with, and we can return before midnight," Steffan huffs, and my eyes flicker between the two of them. For maybe the second time in my life, I'm on Soren's side for this one. Soren's jaw practically cracks from tension, but he resumes his stance, looking bored with life.

I glance at my watch right as the roar of several car tires on gravel fill the silence. "Right on time."

Steffan rolls his shoulders and easily falls into business mode. Doors open and close, and soon about fifteen men fill the space, their leader stepping into the room last. Pierre Locolm's family has spent several years working with The Illicit and offering their ports to our families for shipments out of Louisiana. Having the family on our side could be a huge step for us. Thankfully, my father's tainted business practices have already trickled down to the man, so he knows why he's been invited today.

"Carmichaels." His eyes move between Steffan and Soren before moving to me. "Concord." I watch as he takes a glance at Jose and his lips twitch, "Even a Succo is around these days."

"Almost." Steffan glances at Jose. "Initiation is coming soon."

"That should be interesting." Pierre moves closer to us, and his men file close behind. Although not outright intimidating, I can make out their concealed weapons.

"I take it you've had an opportunity to think about our position," Steffan speaks again to Pierre.

He nods. "I have. It was thorough. I truly have to admire a son who will go against his father to this level." Again, he looks in my direction.

"I would think as a businessman, Pierre, you would see that sometimes having a blood connection to someone doesn't make them a good leader. As the results show, my father has been severely undercutting you in shipment payments." I keep my tone almost bored as I address him, refusing to let him think he will bait me by using my family.

Pierre nods his head and rests his chin on a closed fist. "I want the same deal you gave Diablo."

"Done," Steffan announces.

Pierre turns back to the oldest brother. "I also need help with making a minor problem go away. I'm sure you know what I'm asking for when I say nothing can be left behind."

"I'm aware, as we previously spoke about it. I'll make sure he is treated as well as he treated your own." Steffan reaches forward and shakes Pierre's hand. It looks like we're taking a detour home.

"Where's my good girl?" Soren mutters to the black, inky water, and like a moth to a flame, the water starts to ripple with life.

"It's a little weird how in tune with you she is," I remark, and it earns me a twisted smile.

"Don't be jealous, Lee, just because our girls like me more."

I snort in answer. After our evening together, and my own one-on-one time with Taylor, I have no more worries. For once, I can see the possibility of happiness for us all. It's an image I've been flirting with all day. I can picture the breakfasts in bed, game nights, movie nights, taking her out on dates, and all the possibilities of orgasms between us all. I want the perfect holidays. I want to share her with my best friend and his brother while we twirl her around the dance floor at the Valentine's gala. Even the smallest menial things, such as washing her hair in the shower, are all honors I will gladly take. The possibilities seem endless now that we have her love, and she is secure in our love for her.

Soren can have Allison's love. I just need her loyalty, and in return, I'll keep feeding her her favorite treats. "I think she'd love you more if you presented her with her dessert."

Soren's brow tips up, and he glances at his brother. "Are we ready to let the culprit out of the trunk?"

Steffan glances at the water as the ripples grow wider and more hurried. A large current forms around the beast that owns the waters and the banks. "She's almost here. You should probably get started."

Soren claps his hands almost gleefully before heading to the trunk. "Ready?"

I nod and pull my gun from my side holster and point it at the trunk. Jose moves to the other side where he can't be seen and holds his as well. Soren pops the hood, and sure enough, the idiot tries to escape despite his hands being tied together and the gag in his mouth. The man's face is bloodied and swollen, but I still see the evil in his eyes and can smell the fear on him. I don't care what he did to earn Pierre's wrath. I just want it over so we can go home.

"Don't move," I tell the man, and his head swivels between Soren and myself, and down to the deadly weapon in my hands.

"Take him out, Soren," Steffan calls. "She's here."

Soren reaches for the man, forcing him from the vehicle and pushing his back so he walks. The man stumbles and begs through his gag. Jose and I keep our weapons pointed at him, following them both to the edge of the water. Soren eventually reaches his limit of the whining and punches the man across his face. He staggers backward, and his feet land in the water. Soren keeps going. A punch to the stomach, the face, and finally, a kick to the leg. The man shouts and drops to his knees in the water.

"Bye." Soren gives him a wave right as Allison's large body leaps at the man, tackling him, dragging him under.

We sit and watch her scales as they gleam in the moonlight, her jaws snapping and tearing at flesh and bone. The water turns darker, if possible, with the tinge of blood. The man's screams finally stop and a final bubble pops on the surface. Allison's tale makes a large swish as if to say thank you, before diving back into the water.

"I never get tired of that," Soren says, rubbing his jaw, watching the water.

Steffan scoffs and smacks his twin in the shoulder. "Let's get going so we can get back to Taylor."

"Hey! Remember how I said Chanda is with Taylor. She said to get our asses there now," Jose announces, his cell phone in his hand. "The computer found a match to the hospital where the Angel Maker deaths occurred. It could be a link to our serious problem. So let's haul ass."

Jose is probably more scared of Chanda's impatience than who that match is. I can deal with my sister, but the idea of who the match could be is giving me heart palpitations.

We race back to the safe house on the beach, all of us lost in our own thoughts. I knew there had to be more to the story of what happened. My father has been so intent on hiding his secret. Many times over the next few hours I turn my phone around in my hand wanting to call him, demand answers, give him one chance to come clean about my supposed sibling. I can feel it in my blood that there is something huge we're missing.

It's almost midnight before we pull in and park the car in the garage. I follow the guys up the stairs to find the girls sitting at the kitchen table with a bottle of wine between them. Jose goes to my sister and wraps an arm around her shoulders. Her eyes look troubled when she meets mine. We both want answers, and I'm terrified we might not get them.

Soren meets Taylor for a hug. She stands to wrap her arms around him. He holds her tight before she is passed over to Steffan. I watch as they embrace. When her warm, soft eyes meet mine over his shoulder, I feel the jolt down to my toes. She lets go of him and stands, waiting for me. My body collides with hers, all of her curves melting into mine when my arms band around her waist. I can feel Taylor's heartbeat against mine, and it makes the entire events of tonight worth it. She's here. She's safe, and she's ours.

"I'm so happy you're back," she whispers against my neck, her lips grazing the skin and shivers run down my spine. My arms tighten around her once more before I let her go.

"What did you find?" Jose asks, his hand still clasped in Chanda's. It takes all of my willpower to not glare at him.

"Come look," she tells us, grabbing her wine glass and leading us over to the station we had set up.

"Shit," Soren breathes out, and I follow his line of sight. We all stop and stare at the timeline map we had started. It seems the girls took over that as well. My chest squeezes, though, when I see Taylor's picture in the mix of events and the many lines connecting her picture to other events.

"Little mouse," Steffan glances at her, and I see tears well in her eyes. He reaches for her again, and she moves to stand under his arm.

"I know you all don't agree with me, but it's true. And it's something we all need to look at, take seriously. I know our relationship started at the party and things grew from there. It was fate that I met all three of you, but it is also very evident that because I met you some of these other things happened." She glances at all of us.

Soren opens his mouth to argue, to defend her, but I get her true meaning. "It isn't because of us, or because of you. It's the circumstance. and someone is using our connection to make it difficult for us."

"Exactly," she answers. "I'm not saying this is because of me, or because I'm with any of you. But I am connected to these events and people because we share the same circles."

I look at all the lines and the many different events. Now, some of them are even color-coded. "Why is it purple?"

"It was Taylor's idea that some of these things might have been distractions. Like the alligator and like the time Taylor was chased by the buses," Chanda answers.

"It's a good thing we left you girls here with it then." I chuckle and move to the computer screens. Jose is already typing on the keyboard and flipping through the lists.

"Here it is." He pulls up the information. The lines come up in codes, and he clicks on them a few times before a newspaper clipping pops up along with a deed on the land. "So the hospital used to be St. Joseph Care, named after the patron saint of families. It didn't get converted to a nursing home until fifteen years ago."

"Where does it talk about the child?" Steffan leans closer.

Jose makes a few more clicks to the highlighted line of codes. This time, a certificate of birth pops up, as well as a notification of surrender.

"The mother surrendered that child," Taylor whispers under her breath. I can feel the heartbreak in her words. Shame slithers into my veins imagining my half-sibling being left alone rather than raised with our family. All because of my father.

"Child was born on October thirteenth. Get this, the baby was delivered by Dr. Gutchard and, get this, the nurse? She was the first victim found with the angel wings flayed on her." Jose shifts in his seat and pushes more buttons. "Weird."

"There is no identifying information of the baby, is there?" Soren answers, and Jose shakes his head.

"It's all blank. No hair color, eye color, sex, weight, height, or information on the parents."

"Someone either deleted it, or the nurse knew the information couldn't get out. Which means she knew the baby could be in danger," I guess. "But why?"

"An illegitimate child." Taylor turns to me and Chanda.

"Probably not too surprising but most illegitimate children aren't disposed of. They do run in families, but they just aren't offered high positions," Chanda answers. "So this is different. This mother must have felt truly scared for her child's life."

"There's nothing on the mother. No blood type, description, name, nothing." Jose leans back. "It's just that the birthdate puts the child at the same age as you guys."

"So what? Is my sibling back to take out my father?" I glance around, and then my eyes land on Chanda.

"He would deserve it," she replies, not even caring how she speaks about our father anymore.

"What are you thinking, Lee?" Steffan's head is cocked to the side, but his eyes hold genuine curiosity and hint of concern.

"Dear old dad's days are numbered."

CHAPTER TWENTY-THREE

Taylor

Nightmares plagued me the entire night. No matter how many warm hands grabbed for me, strong arms that held me, or masculine voices whispered that things would be alright, I still woke up over and over again terrified. My mind conjured a poor mother who had to abandon her child because of the fear she felt from The Illicit. The duress she must have felt from Lee's father. I had only seen his parents once at the Valentine's Day gala, and that was enough to send shivers over my flesh. I dreamt of a woman's fear, the guilt that racked her for leaving her child, the brutal understanding that her child was better off without her because of the danger staying with her meant. I dreamt of a child's cries and loneliness throughout their life. Of never seeing the face of the woman who gave them life. One day she was there, and the next she was gone.

I remembered the images of the nurse whose skin had been flayed open like angel wings and thinking she didn't deserve that. Only now I wasn't sure. Did she help aid Amir Concord, or did she do her best to help protect the innocent child and their mother? Maybe she deserved the pain her death dealt her and the bloody crime scene it was.

That's what else haunts me. Blood. The blood in my dorm room, the blood of the homecoming queen, the football player, the images on the news, the torn skin on Chanda's back with the word blood engraved. It was everywhere. Dripping on floors, painted in snow, my hands were dipped in it. All of ours were.

By the time my eyes opened the next morning, I wasn't even sure how long I had slept. I felt as if I spent the whole night tossing before finally being enveloped by love and warmth and that my body had no other choice but to surrender to darkness. My eyes were puffy, and my throat was sore as if I had cried. I did notice I was alone, though, and hushed voices were coming from the living room.

I stand and stretch my exhausted body. The toll this tragic ordeal has taken on our bodies has been physical and mental. My footsteps feel heavy as I make my way to the bathroom. I flinch when I glance in the mirror. "Ugh," I moan. My hair is sticking up in all different directions. A shower will not only fix that problem, but possibly help ease the tension in my muscles.

I feel more like a human after showering the dry sleep sweat off my body and taming my long locks. I brush my teeth, then decide I'm ready to face my guys.

The minute my feet hit the bottom of the stairs, all three sets of eyes land on me. I almost do a double-take when I see the vision before me. Lee is shirtless in a pair of gray sweatpants and cooking eggs in a pan. Steffan is equally undressed, wearing a pair of black basketball shorts while piling a plate full of pancakes. Then there's my dark hero, relaxed at the table in a pair of jeans holding out a cup of coffee to me. I pinch the skin on my arm and wince from the pain. This isn't a dream. This is how every wet fantasy I've ever had comes to life.

"Good morning." My voice sounds hoarse. I clear it before trying to speak again. "What's going on?"

"Making breakfast," Steffan answers with a smirk on his pouty lips.

"Come have some coffee, little mouse." Soren pushes the cup in my direction when I take a seat at the table. "You'll feel a lot better once you have this."

Odd choice of words. "Why is it drugged? Is this a dream?"

Lee snorts and turns with the pan of eggs in one hand and a spatula in the other. "Why would we drug you, babe?"

"I don't know. Since when do either of you cook? And you." I point to Soren who is grinning at me. "Since when do you look so casual like that? You're just offering me coffee without any attitude or crude remarks."

"I'm a new man today." He shrugs like it isn't a big deal.

"Baby, we just wanted to do something nice for you today," Lee adds to the mix and sets a plate full of delicious looking breakfast down in front of me.

"Did something happen?" Panic begins to take hold. Steffan is quick to wrap his arms around me and reassures me in a soothing voice that everything is fine. This seems so... normal. We don't do normal. My suspicion is raised. "What's the catch?"

Steffan full-on laughs at me this time, and sits down across from me and Soren at the table with his own plate full of pancakes and bacon. "There is no catch. We have a few days to lay low. There isn't much else we can do right now about the secret child, or The Illicit. We figured it's a good day to just hang out without school or stress."

"We just wanted to remind you how good things can be with us outside of the bedroom," Lee adds.

"You barely slept last night, mouse. It got us thinking that we need to be better at taking care of you." Soren holds my gaze, and I feel my heart squeeze in my chest.

I want to cry at the gesture, and at the same time, I want to smack them. "You guys aren't the cause of my nightmares. But yes. I think about horrible things happening to you, to us. This is nice. Thank you."

My praise earns me smiles all around. My stomach rumbles, and we all dig into the food. I thought I hit the jackpot before, but now I know that, damn, these guys can cook.

Wiping my lips on a paper napkin, I ask. "What else are we doing today then?"

"The water is pretty warm. We thought we'd go down to the beach, maybe try some surfing and have a picnic later," Lee tells me. Pure glee fills me just thinking about it.

"What about all the security?"

"They'll stay here and guard the house. Jose and Chanda are staying in. They want some quality time without eyes on them." Steffan grabs my hand across the table. "Let's just have fun today."

"I can get behind that," I grin at each of them and go back to finishing up my eggs.

When we're stuffed from breakfast, the guys shoo me upstairs to get ready for our day at the beach. I offer to help clean up, or make our picnic, but all it does is earn me scowls from each of them. I race upstairs and rifle through my bag for a swimsuit. It was a very last minute decision to come here, and I don't like anything I chose. Falling into the bed, my mind wanders to the beach, the hot sun, my guys all around half naked...naked. I sit up and peel off my clothes and throw a cover-up over my body. We're going to be alone. The beach is secluded, and we're not bringing security. I'm grinning so hard my cheeks hurt waiting to show the guys my surprise. Old Taylor would never do this. New Taylor, however, has three men who are in their prime and are underworld royalty eager to bring her to orgasm. Why wouldn't she do this?

When I get back downstairs, they're waiting for me by the front door. Soren takes my hand, and we hop into Steffan's car. He drives us down the paved path until the path turns to sand. I can see the top of the house from this distance, and that is all. If I were to scream, no one would hear me. And I plan on screaming a lot. We cross over the sand dunes and down to a perfectly flat area. The beach is all ours. The white sand feels silky under my toes as we walk to the area Steffan picked out.

He's already setting up chairs and an umbrella. Lee sets down the cooler and picnic basket before reaching for a beer and popping the top off.

"Who is going to help me with sunscreen?" I ask and hold out the bottle in my hand.

"I got this. I'm a professional," Soren jokes and takes the bottle from me.

Lee and Steffan roll their eyes. This is the moment I've been waiting for. My fingers clutch the end of my cover-up, and I tug it off over my head. New Taylor is coming out to play!

"Fuck me," Soren breathes out, and Lee almost spits his beer into the sand.

Feeling brave, I meet each of their shocked gazes with a heated one of my own. "You said it was just us. Were swimsuits required?"

"Nope." Lee quickly says.

"Fuck no, they should not be," Soren answers, and I watch as he flings his own swim bottoms to the ground. His eyes hold a mischievous glint in them when his hands land on my heated skin, rubbing the lotion in.

I glance back up at Steffan and see his throat work, his eyes trailing fire over my exposed body. "Are you joining us or not?" I taunt him. My brazen tone sets him in motion, and soon he is also naked and reaching for me.

"Uh uh." I hold up my hand, my head tilting to the side. "We're not making love right now. You promised me a day to relax. I want to swim and eat and drink and forget about all our problems first."

"Baby, you should have worn a swimsuit then," Lee practically groans while joining us in the nude.

Soren finishes rubbing me down, clearly enjoying himself. “Well, either way we don’t want you getting a sunburn. That’s unnecessary pain. Preventable.”

“And they say Steffan is the saintly one,” I say through a smile.

“Hey. I’m trying to protect you. This is purely for your benefit. You’d think I want to stand here lathering lotion over your nude body all by myself.” Soren’s tone is playful and I love when this side of him comes out.

“I’d be willing to assist.” Lee offers.

Soren gives him the side-eye. “I bet you would. How about you assist in shutting the fuck up and keeping your ass over there. I got this.”

When Soren finishes, I release a squeal of excitement, and before they can reach for me, I take off, running toward the crystal blue water.

Once the cold spray hits my skin, I giggle and scream. I keep going deeper until the water is to my waist before I’m picked up off my feet by a pair of warm arms and slammed into the waves. We both come up laughing and brushing water from our faces. I lunge for Lee next, and he flings me over his shoulder, spinning me as we plunge downward.

We laugh, we swim, we play. My naked body rubs against each of theirs. Flesh on flesh, heat on heat. I can’t manage to take my lips off theirs with needy, greedy kisses as they pass me around in the surf. I don’t mean to, but soon I’m so worked up, my pussy aches to be filled by them. Steffan must see it in my eyes because one second we’re making eye contact, and the next he’s groaning and grabbing my face with both of his hands, dragging my mouth to his and kissing me hard. His tongue invades my mouth, stroking mine, while my legs climb his body, wrapping around his waist.

"Oh fuck, yeah," Soren grunts, his body moving behind mine, his back pressing into me.

"What a good girl," Lee murmurs. His green eyes blaze while he watches Steffan kiss down my throat, sucking and biting the skin, leaving marks.

"Please, I need you," I gasp out loud, and soon we're moving.

Steffan carries me out of the water, over the sand and to our blanket. He drops to the ground and situates me over his lap, the head of his cock pressing against my opening. Placing my hands on his shoulders I raise up and lower my body onto his, sliding down his length. I moan into his mouth while his hands guide my hips up and down, riding him.

"Open," Lee commands and my eyes jump up to him. He's on his knees over Steffan's head, his cock pointed right at my mouth. I open my lips wide and suck him deep. Lee groans in response, his hands fisting into my hair. Soren walks around us, his hand stroking his own dick while he leans in to kiss my shoulder, my neck, and my temple, whispering dirty words and thoughts about the way we look right now. How I'm his good, filthy little mouse. And I am. I can be anything and everything to them.

"Fuck, you suck my cock so well, Taylor," Lee moans and his pelvis hits my nose. I gag around his length and open wider to take in more of him. I love driving him past the brink of sanity.

"Her pussy is squeezing me so tight," Steffan grunts with a lift of his hips, slamming his dick further inside of me. "That's it, baby. Take this dick and milk it dry."

His words set me off, my inner walls contracting around him, my orgasm slams me like a tidal wave. I scream around Lee's cock and soon he's gripping my head, fucking my mouth hard before spilling his own release down my throat. We're all panting when we're done, and I collapse on top of Steffan's chest.

"Go away," Soren snaps at both of them. I sit up and meet his blue eyes that are dark and filled with unrestrained need. I reach for him, and he grabs under my arms, lifting my body off his brother's. Steffan groans when his cock slides out. "Leave."

Lee and Steffan share a laugh and flirty glance before heading toward the ocean together.

"My turn, little mouse," Soren grits before turning me over. My knees land on the sand, and I branch my hands. "Watch them," he commands, and my gaze finds Steffan and Lee in the water, making out with each other. I gasp at the beautiful sight right as Soren plunges his cock inside of me. I scream again, and his hands land on my hips. Soren loves me ruthlessly, bottoming out inside of me every time he surges forward, hips snapping against my thighs. I can feel his heavy sack hitting my ass cheeks, and the thought of it all makes my eyes roll back. I'm full of him, and the angle he tilts my pelvis hits just perfect so that each thrust borders on painful. I reach another orgasm, and this time I'm screaming his name so loudly that the guys are glancing our way.

I collapse right as Soren is calling my name. I can feel his release from every pulse of his cock as he empties inside of me. By the time he pulls out, Steffan and Lee are walking back to us. Soren picks me up and carries me to the water. His gentle side takes over while he cleans us both off in the water.

My legs feel boneless when we start walking back to the others. As if reading my mind, Lee hands me a sandwich from the basket before handing drinks to the guys. Steffan once again pulls me into his lap while we eat.

My body is relaxed, and for the first time in a long while I take the moment to soak it all in. The sun, the waves, the sounds of my guys laughing and talking about things that aren't related to death or blood. I wish I could take this moment and keep us all here and let everything else move on around us. I want this normal. "Can we stay here?"

"What do you mean, little mouse?" Steffan leans down and runs his lips over my cheek. The other two have quieted, and are giving me their attention. Lee reaches for my free hand and runs his fingers over mine.

"When this is over. Or for summer break even. I don't want to leave this place." I can't explain it, but my heart wants the peace I find here. "It feels like home." They fall silent, but I can hear them doing their silent discussions with each other.

"Whatever you want, Taylor, we'll give to you." Soren is the one to answer, and the way he gazes at me makes my body warm all over.

"It's a plan then," I agree.

We spend the rest of the afternoon eating, swimming, enjoying each other, and planning our future. By the time the sun is starting to set we're packed up, and unfortunately, everyone is back in their clothes. Walking to the car has the same effect as the popping of a bubble. We're going back to the real world, and picking up where things have left off.

"Don't there seem to be a lot more seagulls than normal?" Lee asks, his eyes finding the flocks that are circulating above the car.

Steffan glances from where his twin is looking toward where we spent the day in the sun. "It is weird none of them bothered us. We had food and everything."

I watch their white and gray wings as they hover, sweeping back and forth, their loud calls of excitement to one another becoming louder.

"They don't seem calm," Soren speaks, his eyes on the sky. "They're in a frenzy."

Our pace picks up. The closer we get to the car it begins to appear that the seagulls aren't hovering there, but further out. Dread piles in the pit of my stomach, and my gaze lands on the roof of the beach house.

"They're over the house." Steffan picks up on it at the same time that I do.

We rush into the car. Steffan swings it around and starts driving back before we're even situated. My skin starts to crawl with worry.

"Fuck!" Steffan shouts when the house comes into view.

Soren and Lee are leaning out of the car to look. I can't make myself face it, but I see the way. Lee pales and the anger in Soren's eyes. It isn't good. My heartbeat quickens and adrenaline flows in my veins prepping my body to run, hide, and save itself. I swallow back the bile threatening to creep up my throat.

"Call Jose," Lee shouts.

"I am. He's not answering," Soren responds.

My hands move to cover my ears. No. No. No. Not again. Of course this is happening. We were happy. As soon as there's a moment of joy everything has to turn sour.

"Fuck, call the brothers," Steffan orders.

The car slams into park and we scramble out. "Taylor, stay with me. Do not let go of my hand." Steffan grabs my hand, and we're moving over the grass toward the doors. That's when I see it. Red. The ground is painted in it. Blood.

So much fucking blood.

Seagulls feasting on waiting flesh.

My head snaps up, and for the first time I take in the destruction. Even with Soren at my back and Lee prepared to fight next to us as we move through the massacre, I don't feel safe. Bodies are everywhere. Guards, the staff from the house, but what's worse is the two trucks that are vacant in the driveway. Bodies of a dozen brothers from the Delta Pi Theta fraternity are scattered among the others. It was a trap. They were lured here. They were murdered, the slashes to their bodies prove it. One of the men closest to me has his eyes open, frozen in shock.

"Chanda," Lee gasps and takes off into the house.

"Lee!" Steffan calls for him.

I place my hand on his shoulder, begging him not to follow. The front door was already open which doesn't look good for us. Soren bends to check the pulse of every body we pass. I can feel Steffan getting more and more angry as we move slowly toward the side door. The door is ajar and Steffan slowly slides it the rest of the way open, and we move into the house. The air is colder in here, and my skin instantly pebbles with goose bumps. Soren and Steffan open a safe and grab guns, strapping them to their bodies like armor. A vest is thrown over my head and tightly tied to me.

When they're ready, we move down the hall and into the house. Blood is spattered on the walls and floors. My stomach sinks further when we move into the main living space. "I'll check upstairs," Soren tells us.

I want to call him back but remain silent. It looks like they were getting ready to have lunch. Food is scattered in the kitchen, plates piled up. Steffan roams toward the office and sure enough, the computers are destroyed. The carefully detailed map and timeline are shredded.

"Steffan!" Soren calls for his brother.

We rush to the stairs and find Jose propped against him, breathless and severely hurt. "Chanda." He's gasping, his hand holding tightly to his side. Blood gushes around his hand.

"She's not here?" Soren asks him.

"Took her," Jose manages to get out before his legs give way. He slides to the floor, and Soren arranges him on his back. He pulls his T-shirt off and holds it to Jose's side, trying to stop the blood.

Chanda. I look around for Lee suddenly remembering he ran in here before us. “Lee. Lee! Where’s Lee?”

“He isn’t upstairs.” Soren shakes his head.

“Fuck.” Steffan grabs his gun and runs to the basement level. My hands are clamped into fists, my mind still processing the scene around us. I drop to the floor to try and comfort Jose until the medics arrive.

How did they find us? Who did this?

“Where the fuck is backup?” Soren growls.

Sirens are finally heard in the distance. We’re running out of time. How are we going to explain any of this?

“He isn’t here.” Steffan runs back into the room with his cell phone in his hand.

“What do you mean he isn’t here?” Soren snaps at him.

“I mean he wasn’t downstairs, he’s not on this floor, and he isn’t upstairs. Fuck! He isn’t answering his phone.”

My hand covers my mouth, holding in the sob threatening to break free. I can’t lose Lee. We can’t lose Lee. And Jose. Will he get the help he needs in time? Everything is happening in chaos and warped speed but painfully slow at once.

And Chanda. She’s already been through so much and now they’ve taken her again. Lee and Chanda are both Amir’s children. Did he do this?

Steffan backtracks upstairs and to the front of the house. I hear him swear, followed by a loud bang. He storms into the room with eyes full of rage. “His phone.”

Steffan shows us Lee's cell. His voice is raw, and there is a sheen of tears in his eyes.

"Chanda and Lee are missing," Soren breathes out. We're all thinking the same thing. Both of the Concord heirs have been taken.

JOURNAL ENTRY

Unknown author

This is it.
They're here.
And the others will come.
Blood for blood.
I've played enough games.
Time to shed this old skin.
Let's release the snakes.

CHAPTER TWENTY-FOUR

Lee

My head throbs. My fingers tingle. My mind fights for consciousness but keeps blurring with images that don't make sense. I've lost all time and awareness. My body wants to fight. I can feel it in the way my muscles bulge against the bindings. Wait. Why am I tied up?

Blood.

Seagulls.

Soren, Steffan...Taylor.

Chanda!

My eyes pop open, and the world slowly pulls into focus. The memories flood back in a chaotic swirl of color and pain. My baby was crying when I left her to find my sister. My best friend called my name. Jose was on the floor, and then there was nothing else but darkness.

"Oh," a voice speaks, and I fight to lift my head. "He's awake now."

I can feel a presence in front of me. I'm aware of

two other people in the room at my sides. I need to see them. I need to know what is happening.

"Wakey, wakey, Lee." The voice laughs, and I feel the metal of the barrel of a gun tapping my forehead. "Come on, almighty Concord. It was just a small blow to the head."

I manage to lift my head this time and come face to face with a dark figure. He's wearing one of the Halloween masks from our sophomore year. The blue LED lights are lit up, causing an eerie glow. Is he a brother?

"What do you want?" I manage to rasp out, my mouth feeling like cotton balls are stuck to it.

"Me?" The figure laughs, their head thrown back. "I just think this is perfect. Ya know. Cosmic. That everyone is finally here."

"Who?"

The figure moves toward me and bends to my level, I can see their eyes through the slit in the mask. "All of Amir Concord's children."

Panic pierces my heart. My head shifts to the right. Chanda is bound and gagged in the chair. Her head is forward, her long, black hair swirls around her face. All of his children...

My head shifts to the other side, to the other body bound and gagged next to us. Her body is bent at an angle, but I instantly recognize her hair. Fiery red. Noticeable. Just like her.

Kali.

The end.

Die for the Family coming soon...

OTHER BOOKS BY GAIL HARIS

Stand Alone Novels

The Bridge Between Sinners

Arrogant Arrival (A Cocky Hero Club Novel)

Ashes (An Everyday Heroes Novel)

Allegiance (A Salvation Society Novel)

Cleric (Mayhem Makers)

Alluring Serenity (Sunshine Coast Novella)

Gettin' Figgy (A Man of the Month Club Novella)

THE RANDALL SERIES

Stolen Hearts

Forbidden Kisses

Unspoken Desires

K.O. Romance Series

Worth a Shot

My Best Shot

A Clear Shot

Unexpected Ever After Anthology

The Hunkmate

The Sweetmate

The Innmate

CO-WRITTEN GAIL HARIS & ASHTON

THE ILLICIT BROTHERHOOD

Pledge Your Loyalty

Smoke the Enemy

Crave the Illicit

Bleed for the Brotherhood

OTHER BOOKS BY ASHTON BROOKS

The Hearts Duet

Hearts and Bruises

Hearts and Flowers

The Midwest Boys Series

#Rogue (Novella)

#MNGirl

My #MNGirl

#SummerGirl

#NYGirl

The Bedroom Tour

Flawed Heart

Faithful Rhythm

Forbidden Encore (Coming 2024)

Stand Alones

Where Demons Hide

Scar

Warrior (A Salvation Society novel)

ABOUT GAIL HARIS

Murder. Laughter. Happily Ever After.

Gail Haris loves blending romance out of life's everyday chaos. Stories filled with humor, steam, and moments of sweetness, along with suspense and twists.

Using coffee and her imagination, Gail writes in a variety of genres, including romantic comedy, romantic suspense, and new adult/coming of age romance.

Mother of two gorgeous and hilarious girls. Other half to the Boo. Always laughing too loud and thriving on awkward situations, Gail enjoys traveling, binging series, and trying out new recipe (that sounds better than just eating).

Never stop believing in love, dreams, and yourself. And coffee...especially the coffee. Don't give up on coffee and books.

Let's make it awkward: www.gailharis.com

Connect with Gail

WEBSITE

gailharis.com

FACEBOOK

https://www.facebook.com/authorgailharis

FACEBOOK GROUP GAIL'S BOOK BELLES

https://www.facebook.com/groups/gailsbookbelles

INSTAGRAM

https://www.instagram.com/authorgailharis/

BOOKBUB

https://www.bookbub.com/authors/gail-haris

GOODREADS

https://bit.ly/GRGAILHARIS

AMAZON AUTHOR PAGE

https://bit.ly/GAILHARIS

TIKTOK

https://www.tiktok.com/@gailharis

Subscribe to GAIL'S NEWSLETTER
(TWICE A MONTH):
https://gailharis.com/newsletter/

Want to help promote Gail and possibly receive ARCs?
Join GAIL'S MASTER LIST!:
https://bit.ly/GailMasterList

ABOUT ASHTON BROOKS

When love and chaos collide...

Ashton Brooks is an author with a variety of stories that are in Contemporary Romance and New Adult romance. Her writing style is suspenseful and sometimes leads to heart-wrenching conclusions. With a background in forensic psychology she really goes for those investigative, dark and twisty feels. And of course, lots of love!

Brooks enjoys reading as much as writing. Television shows such as Criminal Minds, Scandal, and One Tree Hill are her go-to binge worthy series. She loves spending time with her friends and family with a good glass of beer or wine. If she isn't reading or writing, Brooks is Pinteresting future home projects for her wonderful husband to accomplish.

Follow Me!

WEBSITE:

https://www.ambrooksbooks.com

NEWSLETTER:

https://mailchi.mp/ea5fc7a2a98c/ambrooksnewsletter

Facebook:

https://www.facebook.com/ambrooksbooks/

Twitter:

https://twitter.com/brooksauthor |

INSTAGRAM:

https://www.instagram.com/ambrooksbooks/

GOODREADS:

https://www.goodreads.com/user/show/93577252-a-m-brooks

Join my reader group to get all your info first!

Ashton's Rogue Readers:

https://www.facebook.com/groups/625793331210669/

Made in the USA
Monee, IL
22 October 2023